CHRONOLOGUES
Tales on the Theme of Time

A collection of fiction stories from
Eric Nilles, Chad Olson, Debra Robic,
James Kenneth Rogers, and D.L. White

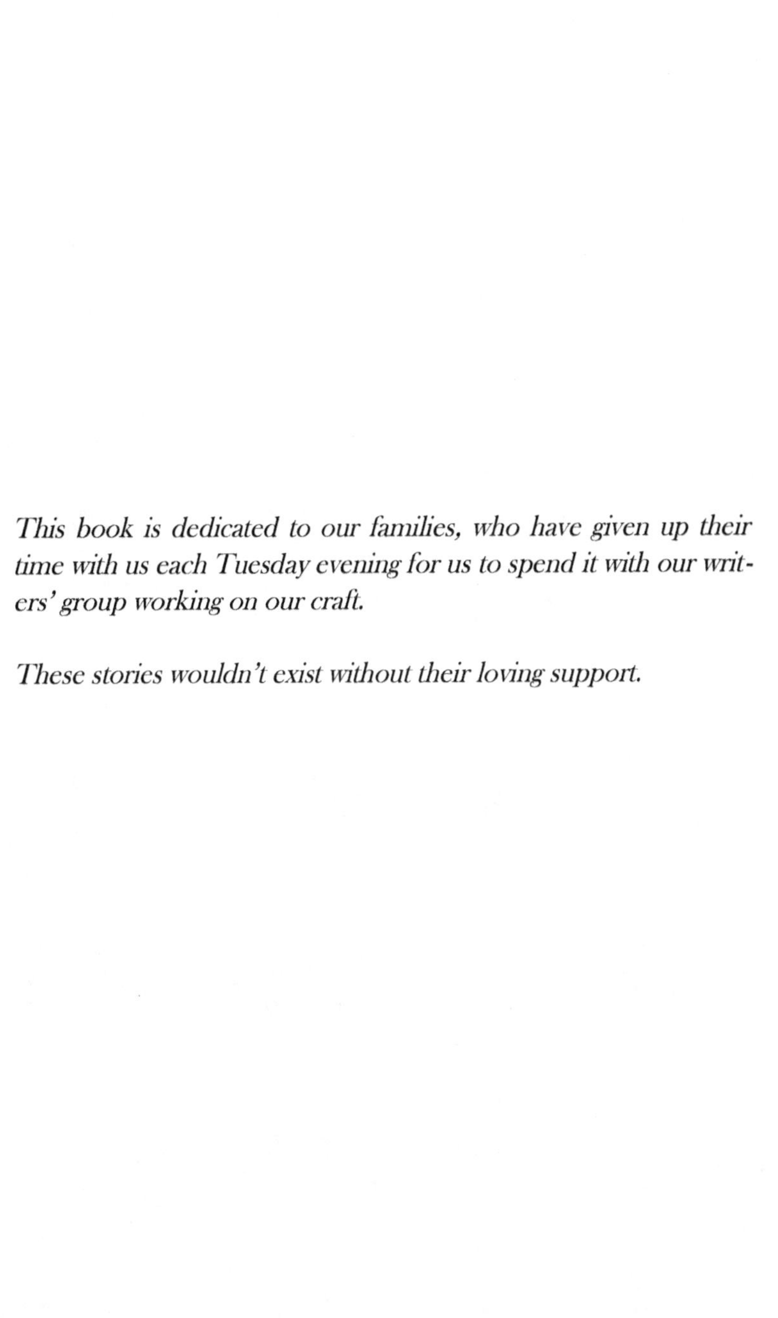

This book is dedicated to our families, who have given up their time with us each Tuesday evening for us to spend it with our writers' group working on our craft.

These stories wouldn't exist without their loving support.

Contents

About the Authors

Eric Nilles was born in Chicago and has lived in the city and its surrounding suburbs his entire life. Currently he lives in the 'burbs with his wife of twenty-six years and their three boys. His early career was spent as an automotive technician and an automotive service advisor, but since 2001 he has been a teacher, where he enjoys imparting his wisdom on the next generation of young adults. His first writing was in the form of a monthly blog he wrote for the automotive industry circa 2005. This series of blogs was mostly instructional in nature and geared toward the average motorist, chock full of advice about winterizing your car, checking the oil, understanding the warning lights on your dashboard and that sort of thing. Soon after, he was bitten by the fiction writing bug, beginning several novels and short stories. In addition to writing, he enjoys working on vintage automobiles, home improvement projects, and playing pinball.

Eric's **"Theatrica Mechanica"** drops the reader into a timeless world of wizards, kingdoms and unusual beasts during a time of great upheaval. The peaceful and the wicked are destined to clash, a peace-loving king will discover he has been granted little time to prepare, and only by enlisting the most cunning members of his court does his kingdom have a chance to prevail.

Chad Olson likes to write weird tales that go unexpected places. He lives with his wife and three children in a suburb of Chicago. He majored in Russian in college and lived in Russia after graduation. He has an admittedly checkered work history. For many years, he was a semi-successful film and stage actor in Los Angeles. To pay the bills during that time (note the prefix "semi"), he worked in real estate development and as a business manager to more successful actors. In a nutshell, he deposited their checks and paid their bills for them. Chad now does government relations work. He enjoys basketball, swimming, keeping up with his Russian skills and writing whenever he has a chance. He has published two science fiction novels, *Stung* and *Invasive Species*, along with several short stories, including "Magic's Price," which can be found at **amazon.com/stores/author/B01G2E0BVK**.

Chad's contribution to this collection is **"The Ladies Three."** Want safe passage for your ship and crew? You can have it. The price the Ladies Three require is but an hour of one sailor's time. An hour, and perhaps something more. But what happens when the sailor selected has plans of his own?

Debra Robic has parlayed writing into regular income for some five decades, working in the technology marketing field. Her real passion, however, is for writing short stories and novels. Inspired by a lifelong love of science fiction, Robic's stories use speculative, imaginative, and sometimes futuristic themes as a lens to amplify and examine the mysteries of the human experience. She takes inspiration from the Ray Bradbury quote, "As soon as you have an idea that changes some small part of the world you are writing science fiction."

In her story **"What If?"**, author Debra Robic invites us to join Sylvia and Alan, involuntary residents of the State old folks' home, as they discover a strange book that asks them to consider: what if they could go back in time and change some things, take a different path here, make a different choice there? If they could, what would they choose to change? And if they did, what would change beyond their choosing?

James Kenneth Rogers writes all kinds of fiction. He's also a lawyer, and when he's not writing, he's busy suing the federal government. A sixth-generation Arizonan, he has lived on four continents. He has four children.

To sign up for his email newsletter and receive a free short story as a thank you, go to

JamesKennethRogers.com/Newsletter.

In his story, **"The Annuity Squad,"** a man who's down-on-his-luck receives an unexpected windfall, and the promise of even more money in seven years. But could it all be too good to be true?

D.L. White has always been writing stories. She received a bachelor's of English from Northern Arizona University and crafting words has paid the bills ever since. She has plied her writing skills in several industries over the years, discovering along the way that the corporate world can suck the life out of you more than any fictional vampire could. So, she broke free from the cubicles to do freelance writing and editing, and to focus on pulling her fiction work out of the shadows and into the light for others to read. She is a night owl and is obsessive about a good cup of tea, as well as a good horror story. She currently lives in a gothic Victorian mansion out on the moors of England where she trains her pet ravens in her free time. Or perhaps she lives in the suburbs of Phoenix, Ariz. with her husband and a very cute fluffy white dog. Either one is entirely possible. She can be found online at **dlwhitewrites.com**.

In **"The Camera,"** she presents a haunting portrait of a young man who is stuck in his grief over the loss of one of his best friends. A story of frozen moments in time, it is a supernatural snapshot of what happens when past regrets turn into an obsession.

Introduction

We are powerless to stop the passage of time.

Yet, we time travel every day.

It's true.

If you've spent time waiting in a doctor's office or at the DMV, you know that time can stretch out for an eternity. Meanwhile, hours spent in a coffee shop, sitting across the table from a dear friend, can seem to pass in the blink of an eye. We hear a song on the radio and are immediately transported back in time to our high school prom. Seeing your bride walk down the aisle at your wedding, time seems to stand still, as you take in her beauty.

We measure our lives in moments. We measure a baby's age in months. Our childhoods are measured by years spent in school, bedtimes, and summer months of glorious freedom. We hold our breath watching our favorite sport, as the game is won in the last few seconds. Deadlines loom at work as alarm clocks wake us up each morning. We segment our lives into the "before" times – *before* I met my husband, *before* we owned the house, *before* the war.

So much of modern literature and film, regardless of the genre, is enamored with the concept of time. In this collection, you won't find any fancy Wellsian machines with spinning brass gears to travel backward or forward through time. There are no sightings of a gull-winged DeLorean that travels back in time once it achieves the speed of 88 miles per hour. But time does play a key factor in each of the stories contained within. Several of our protagonists are challenged to stand up to the test of time, and a few just may find loopholes to its restrictions.

We hope these stories entertain you, scare you, and even make you chuckle a little. We also hope that maybe, just maybe, they inspire you to live out each of your real-life moments with purpose.

May you live a life without regrets. And may some of that time be spent reading a good story now and then.

The Camera

by D.L. White

"It's time, Logan."

"Time for what?"

"Time for you to go grocery shopping," Megan replied.

Logan was seated on his couch. Despite his best efforts to remain absorbed in his smartphone, he couldn't help but hear his sister rummaging around behind him in his tiny kitchen. Half-empty bottles of condiments rattled in the refrigerator door as she shut it.

"There is nothing in here but an egg carton with one egg in it," she noted. "What have you been eating anyway?"

"Hmmph."

Megan walked around the breakfast bar and plopped onto the couch beside him.

"Logan."

"Hmmm?"

He didn't look up at her. He could feel a Big Sister Lecture brewing, and he really wasn't in the mood. He continued scrolling through social media on his smartphone.

"Logan!"

"What?"

Megan reached over and put her hand over his phone, blocking the screen. "I'm worried about you."

Sighing, he turned off his phone and slid it into the pocket of his jeans. He knew Megan wouldn't be satisfied until she'd said her piece.

"I'm fine," he replied, rolling his eyes.

She had stopped by his apartment on her way to the gym, as was evident by her purple tights and an oversized black t-shirt with a silver Nike swoosh on the front. Her wavy brown hair was pulled up into a high ponytail. Megan always looked put together, even while on her way to do something as mundane as working out.

"You're not fine," she said, "so stop pretending like you are."

Megan paused, fixing him with a patient, knowing stare, waiting for him to open up, to expound on his misery. She had learned these tactics from their mother. It just made him want to sink deeper into the couch.

"Why don't you come to the gym with me?" she asked when he didn't take the bait. "Get those good endorphins flowing," she said, slapping his leg playfully.

"No thanks," he replied.

Now it was Megan's turn to sigh.

"When was the last time you got out and took some photos?" she asked.

The birthday party, he thought to himself. *That was the last time.*

"Oh, only every day," he said with full snark.

"I don't mean studio shots of cans of energy drink for a marketing agency or whatever advertiser has currently hired you. I mean *real* photographs. Your art." She tipped her head up, gesturing to the large framed black-and-white photo hanging on the wall next to him. It was a photo of a mountain peak in the distance, framed by pine trees in the midground, with a misty fog hovering along the foreground. He was proud of it, but it was no Ansel Adams.

Logan shrugged in reply.

Megan reached out and put her hand on his arm, a serious look on her face. He looked away from her, down at her hand. Her diamond engagement ring sparkled with the promise of happy days to come - at least for her and Travis.

"I know you don't want to hear it—" she began.

"So don't say it."

"—and I know Hannah was a good friend to you. And I know her death was tragic. But she's been gone for a while now. Don't you think—"

"Megs, just stop—"

"—don't you think it's time to get over it? Move on? I mean, it's not like you two were dating or anything."

"Jeez, Megan!" he said, jerking his arm away from her.

"How much longer are you going to sit in this apartment and mope?"

"What do you care?" he said, standing up. "Besides, Austin says there's no time limit for grief."

"Uh-huh. Okay. But this isn't grief, Logan; it's something more. This is you getting stuck."

"You need to go," he said, feeling his face getting hot. Megan was a carbon copy of their mother - and neither one had ever understood him.

Megan stood up, and he could see tears were forming at the corners of her eyes.

"I know you're just trying to help," he offered.

Megan grabbed her keys off the table and headed for the door. "If you won't talk to me - talk to your friends. They lost her too. Maybe they'll understand this depression you're going through. Because I don't."

He stood in his silent apartment, staring at the closed door, thinking about what his sister had said. She was probably right. But how could he talk to her, or anyone else, about what he was really feeling? The one person that he needed to talk to was gone. What would it matter if he told his friends now? None of them could do anything about it. None of them could fix it.

Logan turned and walked down the short hall to his bedroom and sat down on the edge of the bed. He contemplated crawling under the comforter and going back to sleep. Sleep was the only time he had relief from this crushing sorrow that pressed down on his shoulders and squeezed his heart.

He opened the drawer of his nightstand and pulled out Hannah's funeral program. He read the words he'd read a thousand times before – *A Celebration of the Life of Hannah Marie Nelson.* He looked again through the series of photos of her life, of the time before he knew her. Frozen moments of Hannah - as a child on a swing, her light brown hair flying out behind her, on Christmas morning, hugging the Yorkie puppy she'd begged her parents for, which Logan knew she'd gone on to name Snickers, to her high school graduation, proudly holding up her diploma. Her sweet, shy smile was ever-present in each photo.

Along with the series of family photos, Hannah's parents had used one of Logan's photos in the program – the group shot he'd taken of their camping trip up north the summer after he, Hannah, and three of their friends had graduated from college. In the picture, the twins Jin and Jaelee were standing together. Besides the fact that Jin was a couple inches taller than his sister, they were unmistakably twins, with matching high cheekbones, dark hair, and almond-shaped eyes. Hannah was on Jaelee's left, her arm behind her friend with two fingers up to make bunny ears above Jaelee's head. They were both laughing. Hannah and the twins had been friends since high school, and all three had gone on to attend the same university together. To get the shot, Logan had set the camera up on a tripod with a timer and had run in at the last minute to stand next to Hannah. Austin was on Jin's right in the photo, wearing a red baseball cap turned around backwards, accompanied by his big wide smile.

Logan moved his finger slowly over the details of the photo. Jin's typically spiked black hair was wet and hanging in his eyes. The rest of them looked soggy and disheveled too. Logan remembered the downpour they'd experienced the morning the photo had been taken. The boys had been awakened by the sound of rain and the two girls squealing in their tent next door, as the sudden rainstorm created a running river through the middle of their tent. The guys quickly discovered they'd also done a poor job securing their tent. Running and shoving and laughing, they'd all clambered out of their tents and into Austin's Jeep to wait out the storm. It had been one of those trips where nothing had gone right, with one mishap after another. They'd gotten lost and arrived at the campsite late into the evening; they'd neglected to bring a lantern or flashlights and only had the tiny beams of light on their smartphones to make camp by; and they'd spent their final day trying to get the Jeep unstuck from the mud so they could leave. But the scenery had been breathtaking. And their time together had been special. Often, they would retell the stories of that trip as if it had been the most fun they'd ever had because, strangely enough, it was true.

The three boys had roomed together their first year of college, and everywhere Jin went, Hannah and Jaelee were right there with him. Thus, their little band of friends had been formed. Jin was a very driven, serious student and would be the first one to offer to help you study for an exam. Jaelee, on the other hand, would be the one tempting them all to take a break and go for a hike, to stop and enjoy life. Then there was Austin's warm-hearted gregariousness, and Hannah's quiet, thoughtful kindness. They all just clicked. And Logan had never wanted to disrupt that balance.

He had always believed that no matter what ups and downs life would bring their way - crazy camping trips, the stress of college finals, and more - the one sure thing he could always count on would be his group of friends.

But the aneurysm had changed all that.

His eyes drifted to the obituary printed below the photo: *Our darling daughter, Hannah Marie Nelson, passed away peacefully at the age of 24...*

Was it peaceful? he wondered.

Jaelee had been the one to call him with the news. Hannah had been home that weekend, visiting her parents, and had complained of a severe headache. A migraine probably, although she'd never suffered from migraines. She told her parents goodnight and went to bed early, hoping to sleep it off, but she never woke up.

And yet she looked so alive in the photo, her hazel eyes bright with laughter, one arm around Logan, the other around Jaelee. It hurt to look at it, that singular moment captured in time, never to happen again.

Logan slid the program back into the nightstand's drawer and closed it.

His Canon AE-1 camera sat on top of the nightstand, waiting. It had been a gift from the group, but he knew the purchase had been Hannah's idea. She had been listening when he'd talked about his love of doing "real" photography with 35mm film. She had been listening when he'd talked about the types of vintage cameras he hoped to get one day.

She had listened.

And she had told him about her adventures trying to find it. She had searched camera shops, thrift stores, pawn shops, and more until she had come across a strange little antique shop in Old Town that had exactly what he'd wanted.

He picked the camera up and held it in his hands.

There was a roll of spent black-and-white film curled up in that camera, waiting to be developed. He wasn't sure what was on the front of the roll, but he knew there were three or four pictures on the end from the twin's birthday party.

They were the last pictures he had of Hannah.

He hadn't been ready to see them. Wasn't sure if he was ready to see them now.

But maybe it was time.

* * *

The next day, Logan transformed his apartment's bathroom into a darkroom, something he could do in less than fifteen minutes. Even with the resurgence of interest in film photography, finding a place to get film developed and printed was still tricky. So, a few years ago, after sourcing some equipment, and having Austin cut a piece of wood for him, Logan had devised a way to set up his own darkroom at home. He loved making his own prints and never tired of watching the images float up to the surface of the paper to reveal themselves, like magic.

Logan placed the custom-cut piece of plywood across the bathtub for his work surface. He pulled out the bottles of chemicals, three processing trays, and other supplies from the cabinet under the sink and placed them on the work area. He had done this countless times before, but today he felt these steps had an added weight to them, as if he were performing a sacred ritual.

There was no window in the bathroom to worry about, so blocking the light coming in from underneath the bottom of the door was the final step. He shut the door, shoved a rolled-up towel up against the base of the door, then clicked off the overhead light. He felt a momentary claustrophobia as he waited for his eyes to adjust to the pitch-black room. Once they did, and he was confident the exterior light had been blocked out, he turned on the darkroom light, illuminating everything in a red glow.

Are you ready for this? he asked himself as he stood in the middle of the bathroom, hesitating, cradling the camera in his hands.

I want to see her, he decided.

He took a deep, steadying breath, then rewound the film,

popped open the camera, and took out the exposed roll.

Once he developed the film, it was time to make the prints. Section by section, he placed the negatives into the enlarger. One by one, the images came into view on the photo paper: the rays of a sunset breaking through the trees at his local park, a rain puddle showing a reflection of the Old Town buildings, a POV shot from a hammock showing his jean-clad legs and hiking boots with the tree and forest behind them. They seemed like alien landscapes in the strange red glow of the safety lamp.

Logan felt a growing knot in his stomach as he neared the end of the negatives. He slid the last section of film into the machine and, as he had expected, the last three photos were from Jin and Jaelee's party.

Logan gently rocked the trays of chemical developer and fixative as he moved the prints through the process, then clipped each one onto the drying line. He tucked the light-sensitive paper back into its box and turned off the red safe light. He took a breath, then flipped on the switch for the overhead bathroom light, so he could clearly see his work in its finished state.

The sky-blue tiles of the bathroom walls were covered with black-and-white photos.

He dismissed all the landscape shots; his eyes were drawn to those final three images.

The first one from the birthday party was a wide shot of the group in the swimming pool, as the water sparkled in the sun. Jin and Jaelee were splashing just above the surface, smiling at the camera. Austin was also in the pool, floating nearby in an inflatable swim ring with a puffy cartoon flamingo head on it. He was wearing dark sunglasses and a broad cheerful smile. Hannah was sitting on the edge of the pool deck with her feet dangling in the water. She had turned slightly to look over her shoulder at the camera. At Logan.

The next photo was a low light exposure from later that

same evening, of his four friends surrounding a birthday cake with flickering candles. The small flames made their faces glow in the darkness. Jin and Jaelee were leaning over the cake, ready to blow out the candles, as Austin and Hannah stood on either side of them, smiling, singing the happy birthday song.

The final photo was the hardest one for him to look at. It was also a low light exposure, a medium close-up photo of Hannah sitting on a wooden bench under the veranda. He didn't need the picture to remember it. He had replayed it in his mind countless times. But he was struck anew by the emotions of that moment, confronted with the image of her beautiful face staring at him across time, fixed forever on that bench. The play of gentle light and shadows flattered her features as she smiled for the camera. For Logan.

Why hadn't he told her then? In that moment?

He sat down on the toilet seat lid and began to cry. He cried for all the things left unsaid until there were no tears left.

He reached over and tore off a handful of toilet paper and blew his nose. He felt tired and spent, but a dull ache remained around his heart.

His cell phone began to ring in his pocket. He pulled it out to see it was Jaelee calling and thought about letting it go to voice mail. At the last moment, he decided to answer.

"Hey, what are you up to?" came her bright voice on the other end of the call.

"Not much," he replied.

"Are you okay? You sound weird."

"I'm fine. Allergies."

"Well, I was calling because Jin and I want to try that new Fusion restaurant over on your side of town; why don't we swing by and pick you up?"

"I'm not really in the mood to go out."

"All the more reason for you to join us. It will get you out of your funk."

"That's nice of you. Really. But I think I'll pass."

"Come on, Snaps!" came Jin's voice in the background. He was using the nickname Austin had coined for Logan, short for 'snapshots.'

"Tell Jin maybe some other time," Logan said.

He heard Jaelee move her mouth away from the receiver and relay his message to Jin.

There was a rustling on the phone, then Jin's voice was on the line, "We have reservations for three at six o'clock. So, we'll be there in an hour to pick you up. Plenty of time to get ready."

"But—

"See you soon, bro!"

The line disconnected before Logan could respond.

He stood up, leaned against the bathroom sink, and sighed. He knew Jin meant what he said, and Logan was reluctantly grateful for his insistence he join them. Maybe hanging out with the twins would help.

He needed to take a shower and get ready, which meant his darkroom needed to go back to being a bathroom. He reached up and unclipped a photo from the drying line – an artsy reflection photo of a rainy street.

It really was the perfect shot, he thought to himself, stopping to inspect it further.

He remembered the day he took it. He hadn't thought the rainstorm would stop and had been ready to scrap his day of planned photographic adventures, but the rain had eased up just as he had arrived in Old Town. The puddle was as clear as a mirror, reflecting the 1920s architecture of the buildings that loomed above it.

He could almost feel the chill of that day.

Goosebumps pricked along his arms.

A light blue explosion of color burst out from the tips of

his fingers where he held the top edge of the photo. He watched, transfixed, as it ran like watercolors across the image, filling in the sky, bringing it into full color.

"What the h—" he began to say, then he found himself standing on the street corner of Old Town. He could hear a car horn in the distance as he looked down at the puddle by his feet. A sudden gust of wind cut through his light jacket, and he shivered at the chill. In disbelief, he tapped at the puddle with the toe of one of his red and white Chuck Taylor sneakers. The puddle responded with tiny splashing noises as ripples disrupted the surface.

He looked up, mystified, as he watched a small black bird flapping its wings, fighting against the air currents, as the remaining gray storm clouds drifted across the light blue expanse of sky.

Am I hallucinating?

Logan could hear high heels clicking on the sidewalk. He looked down the street to see a businesswoman in a bright red suit walking towards him.

"Uh... excuse me, ma'am?" he croaked.

She turned to look at him, but before he could say anything more, he felt a tug, like he was falling backwards. His stomach lurched, and he thought he was going to be sick.

He was again standing in his bathroom, staring down at the photo of the rainy day. It was just an ordinary, artsy, black-and-white photo again.

Logan blinked several times.

What is wrong with me? Not enough sleep?

He shook his head to clear it, then reached to take down the next photo, the shot of himself in the hammock. The moment he touched it, his fingertips tingled with electricity, and a vibrant green washed out across the image from where his fingers were, and he could smell pine trees and hear the creaking of the hammock's ropes against the tree trunks. He felt the tipping sensation again.

Logan yelped and flung the photo to the ground as if it were on fire.

It was just a black-and-white photo again.

Did I accidentally get exposed to drugs? Am I high?

He flicked the switch to turn on the bathroom's exhaust fan, then pulled the towel away from the door and opened it.

"Chemicals," he muttered, "Must be."

He leaned against the doorframe, taking a few deep breaths until he felt clear-headed. He hadn't been sleeping well the last few weeks; if it wasn't the chemicals, maybe it was sleep deprivation messing with his head. He promised himself that he would go straight to bed after dinner with the twins.

Logan turned back to the task at hand. He really needed to get this stuff put away so he could get cleaned up for dinner. He was in desperate need of a shower and a shave.

He unclipped the birthday cake photo from the drying line.

She looks so happy, he thought to himself as he stopped to inspect it further. *They all do.*

As he stood there, taking in the image, a golden yellow color burst from his fingertips where he was touching the photo. It ran across the image like shimmering ink, filling in the candles' glow, while an iridescent teal green exploded from the other side, streaking across the photo to bring Hannah's bathing suit into full color. He watched as the flames on the candles began to animate and flicker as—

"—APPY IRTHDAY TO YOU, JIN AND JAELEE! HAPPY BIRTHDAY TOOOOO YOUUUUUUUU!"

"And many mooooooore!" Austin finished, one hand on his chest, the other arm stretched out dramatically to the sky.

Jin and Jaelee leaned forward in unison and blew out the candles on the cake as Hannah applauded.

Logan was no longer in his apartment bathroom. He was standing at the end of the patio table, dumbfounded. He could smell the smoke of the extinguished candles and, under that, the rich scent of the sugar and vanilla of the icing on the cake.

"Happy birthday," Hannah said, leaning over to hug Jaelee.

"Another trip around the sun for me and my former womb-mate," Jin said, pulling out a candle and licking the icing off the end.

Logan heard the neighbor's dog barking next door and turned his head to look out at the backyard. It was nighttime, and the pool lights illuminated the water in the pool, making it glimmer like a turquoise gem in the dark. The pink flamingo swim ring floated across the surface of the water, its inflated cartoon head bobbing comically.

"Who wants a piece of cake?" he heard Jaelee ask and returned his gaze to his friends at the table. Hannah was smiling as she reached across the table to grab a small stack of festive multi-colored paper plates.

"Hannah?" he whispered.

She turned to look at him, her eyes lighting up at her name, but before Logan could say anything more, he felt a tug, like he was falling backwards, and he thought he was going to be sick.

He was back in his bathroom, staring down at the photo of his friends huddled around the cake, ready to blow out the candles. It was just an ordinary black-and-white photo again.

But for a few seconds, he had been back there at that moment in time. Not remembering it, not dreaming it, but actually *there*.

He placed the photo on the counter, then looked down at his feet. He was surprised to see the familiar blue and white tile of the bathroom floor instead of a concrete patio deck. But he was even more surprised to see that he was wearing flip-flops. He didn't remember putting them on. And they were an odd choice for fall weather.

He felt something sliding into place in the back of his mind.

This was no hallucination.

He tentatively took down the next photo, the group shot in the swimming pool. The moment he touched it, a vibrant pink washed across the image, coloring in the flamingo swim ring, and he could smell the chlorine of the pool water as it began to shimmer on the paper.

BANG!

Startled, he let out another yelp, dropping the photo onto the counter.

BANG - BANG – BANG!

It was then he realized the noise was coming from his apartment's front door.

BANG - BANG - BANG - BANG - BANG – BANG!

Someone was knocking loudly and urgently.

As he made his way to the door, he pulled his phone out of his pocket to see that over an hour had passed, and he had several missed text messages and phone calls from Jin and Jaelee.

An hour? But I only hung up with them a few seconds ago.

"Snaps? Are you in there?" came a muffled voice from the other side of the door.

Logan opened the door to reveal a set of very concerned twins.

"We've been knocking for a good five minutes out here," Jin said. He was wearing an exasperated expression along with a black silk dress shirt and pants. Jaelee was standing next to him in a sleeveless maroon blouse and a patterned skirt of white and maroon roses to match. Her maroon-painted lips were pursed with concern.

"I, uh – must have fallen asleep," he said.

"That's a pretty deep sleep," Jaelee said, "Are you okay?"

"Yeah, I uh –," he started to say, then a simple but profound realization clicked in Logan's mind, briefly overriding all other thoughts.

I was there. I can go back.

"Logan?" Jaelee said.

"Uh - I mean, no, I'm not okay," Logan continued, picking up the conversation again, "I think I might be coming down with something. You guys better go on without me."

Jin and Jaelee glanced at each other, with a mirrored twin look he had seen them do before, then they looked back at Logan with concern. He had always wondered if some sort of twin telepathy was going on when they did that but had never gotten up the nerve to ask.

"How about we just stay here with you and order in?" Jaelee offered.

"Nah, you guys have reservations. You should go," he said, starting to close the door.

"Fine," Jin spat as he turned and stalked off to their car, "Come on, we're going to be late."

Jaelee took one step back, then hesitated, "Are you sure?"

"I'm sorry I freaked you out," he said, giving her a weak smile, "Probably a head cold. Really, I'll be fine."

"You'll call us if you need anything?" she asked.

"Sure," he said, "I promise."

* * *

Logan sat down on the edge of his bed and held the swimming pool photo in his hands. Once again, colors of pink, blue, and yellow streaked out from his fingers and across the page, and the water in the pool began to move. He felt a slight vertigo, as if he were tipping forward off the edge of the bed. He blinked and—

— could hear the sounds of the water as Jin and Jaelee playfully splashed each other. He could smell the mouth-watering scent of meat sizzling on a barbeque grill as a waft of smoke drifted past.

"Snaps, you'd better not be burning my burger!" Austin called out to him, bobbing along on the pink inner tube.

"Yeah, watch that food, grillmaster!" Jin chimed in.

Hannah was sitting on the edge of the pool, gently kicking her legs in the water. She turned to look over her shoulder at him.

"Hannah," he called out to her.

"Do you need some help?" she asked, standing up.

He watched, transfixed, as she stood and walked over to him. Alive, breathing, moving Hannah with her shapely figure, her light brown hair dancing in the breeze, and her shy, sweet smile.

"Hannah, I—I have to—" he cried, choking back emotion.

Her brow furrowed in confusion, "What's wrong?"

Logan gasped as he felt the reeling sensation, the feeling of falling backwards, and he was back in his bedroom again, the motionless black-and-white photo in his hands. He could still smell the smoke of the grill.

"Dammit!" he whispered at the photo.

He sat it down next to the other two photos on his bed and stared at them. He decided to try the swimming pool one again and picked it back up.

"Snaps, you'd better not be burning my burger!"

"Yeah, watch that food, grillmaster."

"Do you need some help?"

The events played out just as they had in the past, in the real time of that moment, just as before. Logan tried for a second time to go off script.

"Hannah, I have to tell you something— "

Her eyebrows raised with playful curiosity, "Tell me what?" she asked, handing him a paper plate for the hamburgers. It had "happy birthday" printed on it in joyful colors.

"I want you to know—" he began, then his bedroom spun back into view. His stomach was spinning too, and he thought he was going to retch.

"DAMMIT!" he yelled, slapping the photo back down onto the bed. It was as if these windows back in time were fighting against him, pushing him out before he could alter anything. What kind of torture was this?

He leaned forward and rested his elbows on his knees, waiting for his stomach to stop doing flips. Time travel was not for the weak of stomach.

That's when he noticed the colorful paper plate sitting on the floor.

* * *

He spent several rounds traveling into the photo with the swimming pool and falling back out. Over and over again, he tried to call out to Hannah, to walk towards her instead of waiting for her to come to him. He tried the photo with the birthday cake and got the same results. He finally got the idea to remain inert, to try and not interact with the past, to see if it would allow him to stay longer as an observer, but he was still kicked out at the exact same time.

One one-thousand, he counted the seconds, *two one-thousand...*

"Snaps, you'd better not be burning my burger!"

Three one-thousand, four one-thousand...

"Yeah, watch that food, grillmaster."

Five one-thousand...

"Do you need some help?"

Six one-thousand, seven one-thou—

He always came back after seven seconds.

"Okay," he said to himself, "Seven seconds. You've got to make the most of it."

He stood up to get a drink of water and realized his bedroom was very dark. He reached over, clicked on his bedside lamp, and checked his watch. It was a little after 7:00 PM. He'd only been at it for about an hour.

His phone began to chime, and he picked it up off the bed. It was Austin calling.

"Hey Austin."

"Thank God! Snaps, are you okay?" Austin's concerned voice asked.

"Yeah, why?"

"I've been trying like crazy to reach you. I was almost ready to get in my car and drive over there. Sharon from your office called me. I guess I'm your emergency contact? You didn't show up for work, dude. She was worried. It's not like you to not call in, and she couldn't get a hold of you."

"Why would Sharon be trying to reach me?" Logan said, rubbing his forehead. "Today is Sunday."

There was a pause on the line.

"Snaps...it's Monday night."

* * *

He had explained away his absence to both Austin and his boss by blaming a bad case of the flu, complete with a fever that had made him delirious to the point he'd thought he had called out sick but hadn't. His boss seemed satisfied with this explanation, but he wasn't sure Austin had fully bought it.

He chastised himself to be more judicious with the time he spent with his photos. Just a few seconds in the past amounted to hours in his current day. He hadn't remembered to eat or drink anything and had missed work.

But it was worth it to see Hannah again, even for just seven seconds.

Logan sat on his couch, staring at the portrait of Hannah lying before him on the coffee table in front of him. The only picture he hadn't entered yet. The photo captured the one moment he desperately wanted back, but it was also the one moment he didn't want to screw up. Now that he had a handle on the constraints of the photos' strange magic, he felt like he was ready.

He picked up the print and watched as golden light flowed out of his fingers, washing the photo with color. Logan took a deep breath to steel himself as he felt the room tip forward and—

-- "Can I take your picture?"

It had just been the two of them outside. Austin had gone home, and he could hear the muffled voices of the twins coming from inside the house on a video call to their parents. The string of small Edison bulb lights hanging along the eaves of the veranda cast a soft halo of light around the edges of Hannah's hair, and she seemed to glow against the darkness of night behind her. She had pulled an emerald green sundress over her bathing suit, and her nose and cheeks were kissed a rosy pink from their day in the sun. It had been one of those quiet, perfect moments, and so he had asked if he could take her photo.

"Of course, you can take a picture of me," she said, "You always make me look so pretty!"

I don't make *you look pretty. You* are *pretty,* he had thought to himself, but hadn't said it to her.

Now that he was back, he had another chance.

"It's because you *are* beautiful," he said out loud this time.

Hannah blushed and looked down at the ground, "Oh, that's sweet of you to say."

When she glanced back up at him, he clicked the button on his camera, capturing that open, thoughtful look she had given him.

Logan sat down next to her. He could feel the wooden slats of the bench, hard against his back. He could smell the lingering sweet coconut scent of her sunscreen and the chlorine in her hair. He was back, with her, in this moment.

Just a few seconds, he reminded himself.

"Today was a great day, wasn't it?" she said, looking out at the shadows of the backyard.

Logan of the past had agreed with her when she had said this, and they had laughed together and talked about the upcoming week; all the while he was being eaten up inside with nervousness, trying to will himself to share his feelings for her. And then the twins had come back outside, and the moment had been lost.

"Hannah," he said, taking her hand this time. She wore a purple elastic hair tie around her wrist like a bracelet, and her hand was soft and warm. He never wanted to let go. She looked back at him, startled, but didn't pull her hand away. Instead, she gave his hand a light squeeze in return and his heart soared.

"You're one of the most cherished friends I've ever had —" he continued.

— And he fell back out of the photo, feeling the couch cushions against his back instead of the wooden bench. A gagging sensation crept up his throat, threatening to return his lunch. Logan held up a hand to his mouth, willing his stomach to settle, and realized he could smell Hannah's coconut sunscreen on his fingers.

Only seven seconds. I must be quicker, he said, grasping the photo again as it willingly pulled him into the past. The now familiar world tilted, the cool night air on his skin, back in the moment —

"Of course, you can take a picture of me," she said.

"Hannah," he said, sitting down on the bench next to her and taking her hand. She gave him a questioning look.

"You're one of the most cherished friends I've ever had

—" he continued.

"Oh, I feel the same way," she said with her shy smile.

"And I never wanted to jeopardize that or ruin what our group had together—"

"How could you possibly ruin it?" she asked, her brow furrowing in puzzlement.

"You know, by taking it... by taking us, uh...further..."

His living room came spiraling back into view and Logan cursed himself for being so slow. Once the sensation of vertigo passed, he got up and retrieved a bottle of water from the fridge. He unscrewed the cap and took a few sips to cool his throat and settle his stomach.

These stupid photos with their stupid seven seconds! he thought as he began to pace back and forth in the small kitchen, his mind racing. *Why won't it let me stay there for longer? I want to have all the conversations I never got to have, not just this one. I want to stay there with Hannah forever. Could I stay there forever? Would I die here in this present time if I did? Does it matter?*

He stopped pacing and looked at the other two photos he had placed on the kitchen counter, along with the two items – the flip flops and the paper plate – that had returned with him.

Logan had an idea.

Please let this work please let this work please.

He rushed back to the coffee table to pick up the portrait of Hannah. He felt the invisible cord pull him back down through time—

"Of course, you can take a picture of me," she said.

"Hannah," he said, taking her hand and gently pulling her up onto her feet. Her hazel eyes widened in surprise. "How long does it take to tell someone you love them?" he asked.

"I dunno, just a few seconds," she said, blushing.

"No," he said, "it takes a whole lifetime."

"Oh-kay," she said quietly, looking down at her hand in his. Logan took her other hand in his and pulled her close, and she let him. He felt like they were a bride and a groom standing at the altar.

"I love you, Hannah," he said, trembling. "Will you come with me? I've brought other things through, and I think if you—"

"Logan, I don't underst—"

He could feel the pull beginning at his center, and he quickly enveloped Hannah in a tight hug.

I'll never let you go, he thought, as they fell backwards.

It felt like someone had yanked the living room carpet out from underneath his feet as he re-entered the room. Dizzy, he stumbled and fell down onto his hands and knees, gasping.

Logan sat back on his heels, as the room swayed unsettlingly, and his stomach lurched. He looked around his apartment, praying an excited, hopeful prayer.

"Hannah? Hannah? Are you here?"

There was no reply.

"That's okay," he wheezed, getting to his feet. "That's okay. We'll try again."

He bent over to retrieve the photo from the floor, then paused. A purple elastic hair tie was lying on the floor next to the photo. With a trembling hand, he picked it up and slid it onto his own wrist.

"Okay, okay, we can do this," he said, his pulse racing with excitement. "But no more standing," he reminded himself with a chuckle as he sat down on the couch. He didn't need to risk them both toppling back together, dizzy and hitting the floor hard like he just had.

"Let's do this."

Logan took the photo in his hands and inhaled a deep, centering breath, ready for the colors in the image to come back to life.

But nothing happened.

Fighting to remain calm, he made sure his thumbs were firmly making contact with the paper's surface and focused intently on the image, willing himself into it.

The black-and-white photo of Hannah looked back at him, unmoving.

"No..." he whispered. The photo wrinkled and warped as he tightened his grip on it, "Come on!"

But the image was still and silent in his hands.

He dropped it and rushed over to the kitchen counter, snatching up the birthday cake photo.

"Come on, COME ON!" he commanded the photo, but it didn't respond. Jin and Jaelee were paused in mid-exhale, leaning over their candles. He threw the photo to the ground and grabbed the swimming pool photo. The ripples of water remained static, with his friends frozen in their poses.

"No, NO, NO!" he cried, running back to the couch to retrieve the portrait of Hannah again.

"Please!" he whimpered, collapsing onto the couch, "Hannah!"

The windows back in time had inexplicably closed.

He sat there for hours, the photo clutched in his hand, crying and praying and begging, as he grieved her all over again.

Outside, the world moved on, and the sun began to set, casting a burning orange light through his apartment window.

* * *

Logan awoke from a dreamless sleep and squinted through half-lidded eyes, momentarily disoriented, until he realized he'd passed out in exhaustion on the couch. He rolled from his side onto his back and stared up at the ceiling in his now pitch-black apartment. He felt numb.

A flash of lightning momentarily lit up the room.

When he was a child, he'd been afraid of thunderstorms.

His mother had taught him to count the seconds between the lightning strike and the roll of thunder that followed to determine how many miles away the epicenter of the storm was. It was a good distraction and helped him to feel like he was in control of the danger in some strange way.

Another burst of lightning.

He wasn't afraid now, but old habits die hard.

"One-one thousand, two-one thousand, three-one thousand..." he began to count.

He made it to seven and stopped. He never heard the thunder break.

Another flash of lightning illuminated the room, but it didn't seem to be coming from the window. Now very much awake, Logan sat up on the couch and looked around his empty apartment. He could see nothing but the vague shadows and shapes of his furniture. He shoved his hands into his jeans' pockets, then along the couch cushion, digging for his smartphone to use as a flashlight, but it was nowhere to be found. He stood up and began to feel his way towards the kitchen light switch on the wall when another flash of lightning burst.

"One-one thousand, two-one thousand, three-one thousand..." he whispered to himself as he listened intently, waiting for the thunder to boom. Instead, he heard a high-pitched whine followed by a mechanical clicking noise.

A noise that every photographer knew – the sound of a camera flash and shutter snap.

His breath caught in his throat as he turned to look down the short hallway to his bedroom. He knew he'd left his camera sitting in its customary place – on the nightstand by his bed. Both the bed and the nightstand faced towards the open bedroom door in front of him, but he saw only darkness there.

Maybe the battery or the flash was malfunctioning? he reasoned, as his heart hammered in his chest.

Then the flash on his camera did go off, and for a moment its bright light outlined a dark human figure standing in his bedroom doorway, but it disappeared into the darkness again as the light faded.

Logan blinked furiously to get rid of his flash blindness.

"Who- who's there?" he called out.

He listened for the floorboards or a door to creak with movement but could only hear his own short, panicked breathing.

"Au— Austin? This—this isn't funny, man! Knock it off!"

The camera flash went off again, and the dark figure was closer now, standing in the hallway.

"Get— get back," he said, "I'll call the cops!"

He wondered how quickly he could make it to the knife block in the kitchen, to grab something to defend himself, as he inched backward along the wall.

Another white flash and the shadow figure was standing at the edge of the living room.

Logan's feet were frozen to the floor with fear as he watched the light fade, but this time the figure didn't disappear in the blackness. A white-blue aura began to shimmer around the pitch-black legs, arms, and head of the figure, outlining the edges and features in the dark. The figure was wearing a short white dress that glowed with internal white light as did her hair, which swayed around her face in incandescent waves, set in motion by a wind he couldn't feel. At last, the figure seemed to open her eyes, revealing two white pupils set in a sea of black. It was then Logan recognized what he was looking at, what any photographer would recognize – a film negative, with the lights and darks reversed.

I—I must be losing it, he thought, shutting his eyes to the figure before him like a child, pretending that if he couldn't see it, then it must not be there.

"Looooogaaaaaan," said a faint female voice. It came to him as if echoing up from the depths of an old stone-sided well.

"H—Hannah?"

He forced himself to open his eyes and the glowing version of Hannah was just feet away from him. She was both beautiful and terrible to look at – a strange, blackened angel. She took a clumsy, unsteady step towards him, then another. Her pupils were blazing like white-hot lanterns, yet now he could see the outline of her brow, of her lips, and he could see the sorrow there.

"Loooooove youuuuuuuuu," came the far-off echo, as her lips moved out of sync with her voice.

"I love you too," his voice hitched in his throat. "I'm... I'm s-sorry for—."

"Le------t. Me------. Go------." she said in a reverberating whisper.

"Hannah, please—"

She lifted a finger up slowly to her lips and smiled her shy smile, "Shhhhhhhhhhhhh." Her voice faded away, then her light dimmed and flickered out, and she was gone.

* * *

Logan was awakened by the sound of someone knocking on the door.

He sat up and had a terrifying moment of not recognizing where he was. Disoriented, he took a couple of hitching, panicked breaths until he realized he'd been sleeping on the floor of his small living room. His hands gripped and relaxed across the rough surface of his area rug.

"Snaps?" came a muffled voice from outside, "Dude, open up!"

Logan staggered to his feet, clumsily made his way to the door, and opened it.

Austin, with his big goofy grin, pushed past him and entered the apartment along with the rich aroma of freshly brewed coffee. He clutched a paper bag in one arm and held a cardboard drink carrier in the other hand with two coffee cups nestled inside.

"Bagels and baseball with the bros!" Austin said with sunshiny happiness. He had always been a morning person, bright-eyed and bushy-tailed.

"Wha—?" Logan asked, still feeling dissociated from the world around him.

"It's Thursday, dude. And we've got a date with the batting cages. Let's carb up and get going... As long as you're feeling better, that is."

"Thursday?" Logan muttered.

Austin set the food items on the kitchen counter and began to pull out a bagel and a small carton of cream cheese from within the paper bag when the photos on the counter caught his eye. Logan watched as Austin's gaze roamed up and across the room, taking in the sight of black-and-white photos scattered everywhere: on the counter, the table, the floors. A kitchen chair had been overturned at some point and the coffee table was at an odd angle.

"Everything okay here?" Austin asked in a calm, measured tone.

Logan picked the kitchen chair up off the floor, righted it, and sat down. He rested his head in his hands. "You wouldn't believe me if I told you."

"Aww, try me," Austin said, bringing the food over to the table to join him. He shoved a cup of coffee and a bagel at Logan.

"I think..." Logan began, "I uh..." He looked to his left, down the short hallway to his bedroom, where his bed remained tidy and unslept in. The camera was sitting, quiet and still, on his nightstand.

Austin sat down in the chair across from him and stretched. He took off his baseball cap and hung it on the post of the chair behind him.

"Dude, we've all been worried about you. Me, Jin, and Jaelee," he tore off a piece of bagel and munched on it as he talked. "They told me how you were acting all weird. Blew them off for dinner. Plus, you're missing work. You're not talking to anyone."

Austin had completed his master's degree in psychology and was currently working towards his doctorate while also doing counseling work at the Student Center. Logan wondered if Austin was here looking for a thesis topic. He could see the synopsis now: crazy man obsessed with dead girl thinks his camera is magic.

"I don't need you psychoanalyzing me," Logan said.

"Really, dude?" Austin said, frowning, "I'm here as your friend."

He could tell Austin was genuinely hurt by the implication. Logan looked down at the bagel on the table in front of him, ashamed.

"Come on, just tell me what's going on. Let me help."

Logan glanced down the hall again, then looked back at his friend.

Austin gave him a reassuring smile around another bite of bagel.

"It's Hannah..." Logan began, but his voice caught in his throat, unsure what to say next.

"We all miss her," Austin said in a quiet voice, leaning forward and resting his elbows on the table. "It just isn't fair."

Logan took a deep breath and said, "I... I loved her." It felt strange to hear the words out loud.

"I know, man. Hannah was the best," Austin agreed. "We all loved her."

"No, I mean... I was... I was *in* love with her."

"Oh," Austin said. He thought for a moment. "And you never told her."

Logan shook his head.

Austin leaned back in his chair. "Damn."

"Yeah."

That simple truth had been hard to share, but it felt good to confide in Austin, so Logan decided he might as well press on - although his next admission was a whole lot weirder.

He took another deep breath and said, "I think... I think Hannah's ghost is trapped in my camera. And I... I think I trapped her there."

"Okay," Austin said, with a simple tone of acceptance, no judgment. He took a sip of his coffee.

"So, I'm crazy right?"

Austin shrugged. "Do *you* think you're crazy?"

"I... I don't know."

"Grief can be a powerful thing," Austin said. He tore off another piece of bagel and slathered it with cream cheese. "In fact, it's normal for grieving folks to think they hear or see their loved one who has passed. Part of the brain's way of processing the loss. Like expecting them to be there and trying to get accustomed to the new normal of not having them around."

"I... uh... yeah. That's not what's happening here. This is different."

"Alright. Tell me more. Why do you think she's trapped?"

"I've heard her voice. Coming from the camera. All night," as Logan talked, the words began to tumble out of him faster. "She's inside the camera and she's crying and begging me over and over to let her go. It was an accident. I didn't mean to... I didn't know..."

"Okay, deep breath," Austin said, "Take a minute."

Logan took a deep shuddering breath and let it out. His hands were shaking.

"You don't believe me."

"I believe that *you* believe it. And that's enough for right now. Why don't you back up and start from the beginning?"

So, Logan relayed the events of the last couple of days to Austin. He told him about the photos being portals back into actual time, how other items had come back across time with him, and how he'd tried to bring Hannah back too.

"But it didn't work and now I think she's trapped between the past and the present."

Austin nodded, considering all Logan had told him.

"So...uh... what do you think I should do? Check myself into a psych ward or something?" Logan suggested with a nervous laugh.

"I think you should listen to Hannah," Austin said. Logan searched Austin's face for the appearance of his trademark prankster grin, only to discover he was being serious and thoughtful. "I think you should let her go."

"Ok...uh...how do we do that?"

Austin shrugged. "Maybe you need to get rid of the camera. Destroy it."

The suggestion of destroying the camera made Logan uneasy, but the gears began to turn in his mind.

"Let's go back to the source," Logan said, "Let's take the camera back to the store. See what they have to say about it. About its history. Maybe I can get some answers that way?"

"Okay. I'll help you," Austin said, clapping his hands together. "Let's Sherlock this thing."

* * *

Logan pulled down the cardboard box from the shelf in his closet and set it on his bed. He lifted the lid and began to remove each one of the items from within: the strap and protective carrying case for his camera, an interchangeable lens, the instruction manual, a red envelope containing a happy birthday card the whole gang had signed for him, and finally, a yellow receipt from Leland Antiques and Collectibles, where Hannah had bought the camera. Always thoughtful, she had included it for Logan in case there were any problems with the camera and he needed to return it.

When his calls to the phone number on the receipt went unanswered, and nothing showed up in Austin's online searches for Leland Antiques, Austin suggested they take a drive to the location.

"And bring the camera with you," he said.

Logan put the camera and all its equipment back into the box and carried it out to Austin's car.

As Austin drove to the location shown on the receipt, Logan resisted the urge to look over his shoulder at the camera in the backseat. It crouched there, ominous. He kept waiting to hear Hannah's anguished cries or to see the flash burst and reveal her ghostly image. But the camera remained quiet and inert in its box.

Once they'd reached Old Town, Austin pulled his car up to the curb and parked.

"Dude, read the address to me again?" he asked, opening the map on his smartphone. "Because this is supposed to be the place."

Logan read the address to him.

"Bummer," Austin replied.

They both looked out the window to see an empty dirt lot in between an automotive repair shop and a convenience store on the corner.

Unwilling to let it go, Logan opened his car door. "Let me just check. See if the folks in there know where the shop might have relocated to."

"Want me to come with you?"

"Nah, I'll only be a second. Stay here and make sure we don't get a parking ticket."

Logan pushed open the door to "Mama's Market" and a little bell on the handle gave a pleasant jingle to welcome him. He decided to grab a cup of coffee from the carafe on the counter next to the prepackaged pastries, then approached the register. An older woman was sitting on a stool behind the counter, her salt and pepper hair hung in two braids on either side of her head, and bright, pink-framed half-glasses were perched on her nose.

"Excuse me," he said, approaching the counter and setting down his paper cup, "have you worked here long?"

The older woman behind the counter chuckled as she rang up his coffee, "Honey, this is my place. I've always worked here."

"So, you're 'Mama'?" he asked, smiling as he pointed towards the street sign outside.

"I sure am, darlin.' What can I do for you?"

"I was wondering, when did the building next door get razed?"

She gave him a perplexed look. "The auto shop? It was still here this morning when I got here," she said, leaning back to look out the foggy window.

"No, the antique shop next door. When did it shut down?"

"Ain't nothin' been there for years except an empty lot. And I've been here for goin' on twenty-some-odd years now."

Logan felt a chill crawl up the back of his neck.

"Oh, I must be thinking of another street," he offered.

He thanked Mama and stepped back outside into the crisp fall day. He stood there for a moment, considering what she had said. The breeze made shushing noises through the trees lining the opposite side of the street. The sound was oddly comforting.

"Okay," he said, resolving himself, "It's time."

He walked back to Austin's car.

"What did you find out?" Austin asked as Logan opened the car door.

"Nothing."

Logan reached into the back seat to retrieve the cardboard box with his camera and all the equipment.

"Then what are you—?"

"Just give me a minute," Logan said.

He walked to the center of the empty lot and set the box down next to a tuft of weeds and yellow dandelions.

"I can't keep chasing this. Chasing you..." he said, trying to bolster his resolve. "It's time to let you go. I understand that now." He knelt down on one knee and rested his hand on the lid. He took a deep breath. "I hope you can hear me."

"Goodbye, Hannah," he whispered.

Suddenly, the box felt warm to the touch. He pulled his hand away just as a blue-green flame licked out from underneath the lid. Logan stepped back, holding his breath in amazement, and watched as the flames grew and the cardboard box blackened and curled in on itself. He heard a loud crunching sound, maybe of the crystal lens shattering, followed by a metallic *ping*, as if one of the springs or gears inside the camera gave way in the heat.

He forced himself to turn away and walk back to the car.

"You okay man?" Austin asked as Logan got back into the vehicle.

"Yeah, I pulled my hand away before it could burn me," he said.

"What are you talking about?" Austin asked, giving him a perplexed look.

"Didn't you see? It caught fire all on its own."

Austin leaned forward to look past him towards the vacant lot and Logan turned to follow his gaze.

There was no sign of a fire.

And the cardboard box was gone.

Follow the author and sign-up to be notified of new releases at **dlwhitewrites.com.**

The Ladies Three

by Chad Olson

"'Tis but an hour, lad," Eben said, securing my wrists behind me. "Me and the other men won't soon forget this service." He gave the fetters a final tug. The leather straps bit into my skin.

I leaned my head back against the mast he had tied me to and took a deep breath. It was time. The waiting was over. My stomach felt like I was leaning over the edge of a precipice. The ship rolled and creaked underfoot. But that was not the reason for the disquiet in my stomach.

Above my head, against the night sky, the sails flapped lazily, caught in fitful competing gusts running first one way, then the other. The rigging knocked against posts with repeated, desultory clacking. Our ship had slowed to a crawl, though the waters we navigated were choppy. A sudden large wave slapped the ship and salty spray stung my dry lips. To my ears, the ocean sounded hungry. A roaring lion.

Apparently satisfied with the knots at my wrists, Eben limped around the mast to face me. His apologetic smile looked more like a grimace and did little to put me at ease. He was the last of the sailors on deck besides me. The rest, thirty-one men in all including the captain, were huddled in the hold below to wait out what was to come.

"Now then, test those ropes to make sure they're good and tight. You don't want to get loose."

Obediently, I tried pulling my arms apart. "The rope's tight," I said. I kicked up my left leg. I looked down at the length of rope tied to my left ankle. "I am good."

The old sailor shook his head. "Never had someone specially request rope at his ankle be tied just so. Hanging loose like that, it won't do much to save you if the Ladies somehow get your arms free. They've been known to, once or twice."

"This works for me."

Eben laughed, a bitter sound, devoid of pleasure. "As does that strange blade tied to your arm? Oh, don't look surprised. I saw you strap it there, thinking no one was watching you and felt the handle just now as I tied your wrist. Won't do you any good. Every man has a strategy with the three sisters, and then he meets them face to face. Will you tell me your reasons behind this loose rope at your feet, only one ankle tied, and this blade made of bone, I think it is?"

He waited.

I outwaited him.

"Well, we don't have time for you to just sit and stare at me. It's what you're good at, after all. Lord knows, you done it to all of us these past months. The odd boy, late to sign for the ship, a boy no one knows, quiet as a clam, his lips shut just as tight. That's the reason many of the men..." he trailed off, shrugged his shoulders in a resigned way. "Wasting my breath, I s'pose."

He took a different tack. "Lad, you know I like this not at all. I pled your case afore the captain but he would not be put off his decision. And it don't help none that you volunteered. How old are you?"

I looked up at the fast-moving clouds scuttling past a snow white full moon, not able to meet his eye. "Nineteen."

Eben tsked. "You're fifteen if you're a day. Look at me, boy. There are no answers up in that sky this night." Our eyes met, and his were narrow, appraising. "Well, you got the green eyes I hear the Ladies like, and you're young, so the hope is they'll be merciful and take something small. I would like to stand in your place. But you know they've already seen me and taken a token." Both of us looked down at the black knob of wood where his foot and ankle should be. "No, the Ladies would be put in a rage if they were to find me lashed here, and like as not would pull the ship down to the bottom out of spite, killing us all."

I squared my shoulders and felt the leather straps bite deeper into my wrists. "I said I would do it, and I meant it. Mayhap the men will trust me now."

"Trust you, trust you. Aye, lad, mayhap they will." He put shaking hands up and adjusted his cap. Then he stole a glance at the approaching fog. Over the sound of waves slapping the hull, I heard him muttering, "Sending just a lad...murderous fool of a captain...will kill us all." His eyes found mine again and he cracked a smile. "With the Ladies, be courteous, polite like. You seen how Seaborne acts?"

"Tetched in the head."

"Aye, he is, a bad encounter with the Ladies and never been the same for it. They take something from every man. Sometimes it's a small token, sometimes large. Woe to him, they stole his sense. A heavy price. Now, I've no doubt you've seen the way Seaborne twists his sheets into knots every night, murmuring nonsense, always restless in his sleep. 'Tis a sad thing. But knowing what he was like afore he met the Ladies, I'm imagining he wasn't enough of a gentleman to the sisters three and the toll for that kind of behavior was high." He shook his head and rubbed the sparse gray whiskers that roughened his cheeks and chin. "Ah well. Nothing for it. Seaborne, he done his duty and now you must do yours. That's sometimes the price for a ride on the Sea of Sorrows. Follow the rules. The Ladies will be kind as kittens if you abide by 'em. Now, you remember the words to say?"

"I do."

"Well, repeat them now an' keep an old sailor happy. Miss not a syllable, give the tribute they demand, get us safe through the Ladies' storm, and Cook will treat you to a real meat dinner, I dare say. Captain may even host you at his table. A real honor, that. I only been at his table once myself. Now, say the words and then I must take myself below."

I did not think the captain's table would be that much of an honor and, truth be told, I would rather be in the hold with the others.

I wished it were the captain up here instead of me, no matter what promises I had made to my mother. The captain was the fault-finding, diminutive sort that commanded no respect, only receiving obedience because of the pain he could inflict. He was fearsome generous with his whip, which he always clutched in his right hand. He made the sailors grumble behind his back, and we all thought mutinous thoughts. Of course, it would do no good to tell Eben a sentiment about the captain both of us already knew, so I held my tongue on the subject.

Eben eyed me expectantly with his hands on his hips, and I realized my thoughts had taken me from the task at hand. A bad trait I'd had since I was very young. Eben would not leave until I repeated the words they'd drilled into me the last few hours. I had known them already, having learned them from my mother's careful instruction, but I had feigned ignorance during the sailors' panicked, intensive tutoring.

Acting as if I was resigned to it, I opened my mouth to repeat the incantation when a heaving wave struck the ship. Seawater wetted Eben's back and legs, making him shout in surprise and stumble toward me. He steadied himself on the mast at my back.

Eben, shivering, leaned in close. His breath smelled of stale tobacco. He put a hand on my shoulder. "This gives me no joy, my boy. Know that well. Now, tell me the words and I'll cease bothering you. If any of us are to survive this, it must be but a single soul on the deck. That wave there was the Ladies way of telling me to be on my way. Now, the words, boy!"

I nodded and looked up at the moon instead of into his wrinkled face because the silver light above put me more in the mood of a prayer.

"Ladies numbered Three,

Hearken unto me,

be ye welcome on this ship,

I beg safe passage through the storm,

pray bid this sea to loose its grip,

to keep these sailors safe from harm."

Eben, who had mouthed the words with me, grunted, pleased. "I'll leave you to it then." He held up a single finger. "One hour. The captain will turn the glass when I get below deck. The Ladies only ask an hour of a man, and you can make that with minutes to spare, my boyo. Why, I've seen you climb the rigging like a regular fearless monkey, and swim in roughened sea like a seal. No, you'll have no problem doing this little task. You're finely made, and the Ladies won't want to mar God's good work. One hour is all we ask, lad."

"I'm doing my duty. I said I would."

He peered at me, perhaps a kernel of suspicion still lingering since I had volunteered to face the three sisters. When I raised my hand for the duty, Eben took me aside and told me it had been the first time he had ever heard of anyone doing such a thing. Usually lots had to be drawn and fights occurred to avoid it at all costs. The other sailors and the captain had been relieved at my willingness, but old Eben had got to wondering, and I could see in his eyes he was wondering still.

But now time was pressing, and Eben wouldn't be solving this mystery before the sisters arrived. He turned and limped away, the *scuff bump scuff bump* of his steps thunderous and somehow more forbidding than the sound of nails driven into a coffin. He paused at the door that led a body down to the hold and turned back. Out of the direct moonlight, the wrinkles in his face deepened, as if they were canyons cut into his skin, and his eye sockets were shadowy black holes.

"Know this afore I go down. Every man below, every single man, is depending on you. Think on that when the temptresses' tongues are in your ear. We're counting on you, lad."

"I hear you," I said. "Tell the men not to fear," I lied.

I hated lying to Eben. The rest of the men, and certainly the captain, mattered less to me. I was putting them all at risk this night. But this they could not know.

Eben nodded one last time, tugged the hold door open and, perhaps scared of any more time on deck with the Ladies fast approaching, he slipped inside quick as a mouse into its hidey-hole.

I took a deep breath and stared out toward the bank of green fog a mile off to the starboard. The domain of the Ladies, this fog was the harbinger of their appearance. Any ship that sighted the fog knew what it portended. The Ladies were coming - prepare. One sailor would be required to greet them, offer the requested token, and plead for safe passage across the Sea of Sorrows.

Usually, such a man lived to tell the tale, though some did not.

When the green fog had been sighted six hours ago, a groan of despair had sounded from every throat. Every sailor of these seas knew a visit from the Ladies was possible, but hoped against hope that a ship could avoid it. The captain, his breath coming in wheezes as he capered about the deck nervously, had found the special hourglass for the purpose of calculating the Ladies' arrival. He flipped it for the first time. All knew, at the end of the sixth upending, the ship would be enveloped by the mist, and stay fixed in place for that hour, becalmed, even as rough waters raged about.

The green fog swirled closer, eating up the distance with a

ravenous appetite. The hour was at hand and I imagined the captain, old Eben and the rest of the crew watching by candlelight as the final grains of sand poured through the narrow opening in the hourglass. They would flip it this final time, the seventh time, my time, and wait.

My breath now came fast as I knew the Ladies were closing in. I picked up a new scent mingling with the salt of the sea - roses. I blinked and saw...it was as if I were a child again, taking a walk in my mother's garden and the heavy blossoms were swaying in the wind, some with longer stems dipping down to kiss the dewy grass. I stooped and I was cupping a yellow flower in my hand, just now opening to the sun. I leaned in gratefully and its petals were as soft as a baby's skin against my nose and cheek, and its smell almost made me faint dead away.

My eyes snapped open. Awareness of the here and now returned. My mother had grown a garden, yes. But she had also given me a task. I must not succumb to the Ladies' spell, and lose all willpower of my own, in the very first minutes of their arrival.

Free from the glamour she had cast, I saw the first of the Ladies pulling her hand back from my cheek. Ah yes, the beauty. My mother had told me about her. Naturally, I had not seen her approach under the influence of the glamour, and now she was simply there, before my eyes, lit like she had a candle burning within, making her skin glow golden yellow.

She regarded me with a slight, inquisitive smile. To look at her was to see beauty that was somehow terrible to look upon - like staring into a desert sun. With high cheekbones, tiny nose, smooth wide forehead, eyes like limpid green pools, lips like two hearts conjoined. After only a few seconds, I forced myself to look away and stare down at my feet on the deck. She was too beautiful, and someplace deep inside I felt the animal part of me panic, want to flee, get as far away from this beautiful alien creature as I could. But I also longed to look at her. Look at her forever. Drink her in. The deepest parts of me wanted to look into her face and have her take me to that garden with the roses. I struggled and felt the straps binding my wrists tear deeper into my skin. I wanted to circle my arms around her with everything inside me.

I gave up, spent, and my breathing came out in gasps.

Tinkling, beguiling laughter like the sweetest bells. My head jerked up, but I kept my eyes off her face because I felt that to look even once more into her eyes was to tempt fate. Instead, I fixed my gaze on her stomach, which I could see through the flowing translucence of her moonlight white gown. The small dot of her belly button drew my attention. Even that small feature of her body made me ache to place my hand upon it. I imagined how smooth and warm her skin would feel. *Oh, Mother, I did not think it would be this difficult.* The prospect of failing my mother was like a dash of cold water in my face.

I shouted in defiance and the lady before me laughed again.

"Sisters!" she cried out. "How the boy shouts his defiance. Glorious! Come see his eyes. They are as green as mine. As green as the sea. What a morsel is he. Such sweet respite from the brine."

All at once, the ship listed starboard.

My mother had warned me what I would be seeing this night should it chance to come. But no words, told to me as a boy at her knee, could have prepared me for the dread appearance of the second Lady.

At first, all I saw was a webbed fist clutching the edge of the deck. Then, the ship jerked downward again, and something flew over the side of the ship toward me. In this blur of motion, I saw whatever it was measured three or four times my size. It was light gray in color, spewing red liquid, some of which struck me in the face. Completing an arcing course through the air, it landed with a dull wet *thwack* on the deck not ten feet from me. I realized with a start that it was the lower body of a dolphin. The head was gone, recently torn away, for I saw more of the blood that had struck me a second ago stream out from the twitching headless trunk.

I felt the contents of my stomach stir with disquiet and rise up, burning the inside my throat. I wished with all my heart to wipe my face clean, but could not.

With difficulty, I swallowed the bile and looked back at the sister who must inexorably be following the meal she had flung onto the boat. Beside the fist, a webbed foot with black talons crowning every toe hooked over the side of the ship, making the wood whine in protest. With a grunt, the second Lady pulled herself upward, and her head emerged from the deep and over the edge of the ship.

I closed my eyes but felt the sickening lurch as a large body at last rolled onto the deck.

A voice that was more of a whisper said, "Ah now, lad, look on me, meet my eyes, lest I be offended."

Gray, sagging skin clung to the bony body of a giantess born to swim the deeps. A smell of an ancient swamp, where dead things linger in stagnant water, enveloped me, overwhelming any other sensation and making my gorge rise once again in my throat. Lank brown hair, braided with kelp, framed a lantern-jawed face. She opened her mouth in what I could only guess was a smile, perhaps in greeting, and her teeth were rows of tiny needles going back and back into a throat that didn't seem to end.

A tongue lashed over the rows of teeth, "Hello morsel," she hissed, then added: "Such eyes."

"I told thee true," affirmed the beautiful sister. "But where is our last sister?"

"Late as always," came the whispering reply of the giantess. She thrust a hand down and grasped the dolphin by its tail.

With a flick of her wrist, she brought the upper body of the animal to her mouth. Though I closed my eyes, the sound of tearing flesh and bone did at last make me empty my belly.

More tinkling laughter. "Mind your manners, dear sister, lest the boy faint away. Where could our last sister be? Gone astray?"

The ship heaved up, as something immense pushed up from the deeps, and the entire vessel shook from stem to stern. The impact caused the mast to knock hard against my head. I saw stars and had to fight to stay conscious. Above the deafening roar of rushing water, I heard the same, ever-present tinkling laughter, as if the first beautiful sister had taken up residence inside my head. I coughed and spat the salty brine out of my mouth and blinked my eyes. The ship slid to the starboard at a terrifying angle.

All at once, the first sister's cool hands were there, trying to soothe me, pushing the hair back from my face, curling it around my ears.

"Just a moment, darling," the beautiful one said. Subtle as a cat, she had maneuvered behind me without my seeing. "Our last sister has arrived. You will see her soon. Ah, it would have been so much sweeter for me if you'd stayed in your garden with me. So much sweeter." I felt her teeth nip at my earlobes. I tried to look back at her but she suddenly gripped my head fast, and positioned it so I had to look straight forward.

The giantess cackled, pointing a black talon at me. "He'll hear her soon enough. She's coming up now."

For a moment, all was silent. The sea itself seemed to pause in expectation. The ship's ever-present creaking, the whining of ropes, the metal clasps – all of it gone in this strange pause. And then, a tone sounded, seemingly from far off and so quiet at first as to be hardly discerned. But something within me cried to hear more. As if in answer to this desire, the sound rose quickly in urgency and pitch, always seeming to ascend. Always seeming to rise up to the rafters of my ability to hear, and I was spinning with it and struggling once again against my bonds, frantic, the music, such music, was calling me and I needed to run to it. I knew nothing of the bonds, nothing of the mast that must still be at my back. I knew only the persistent, wonderful, aching call. I could not wait to go to this voice, the song of the last sister. I had to run for the edge, plunge over, kiss the sea, dive deep and find her, have her welcome me into everlasting, glorious sleep. Give her whatever she asks. Give her all of me if she asks it.

"Let me just get you free..." I dimly heard an amused, tinkling voice say. "These knots were done well." A tugging at my wrists. She mustn't find...something. I couldn't remember what exactly, though I knew it was important. I heard myself howling, making hungry noises I knew to be coming from my throat but didn't recognize as human.

"I almost have you free," she sing-songed.

"Let me...let me...go to her!" I shrieked. Was that truly my voice?

"All in good time," said a rougher voice, chuckling, chewing on something. The ugly sister. The eater of fishes from the deep. A loud swallowing sound. "Ah," she continued, her mouth now free to speak, "Sister's voice is glorious this night."

What were these others with their guttural words when she...*she* was calling me with her music that promised all satisfaction, all comfort, forever sleep?

The bonds at my wrist gave all at once, I flew away from the mast, toward the front of the ship. I almost reached the edge, my steps frantic, before my right leg jerked, something tugged at my ankle, and I collapsed onto the deck, knocking my head onto the boards.

"What's this?" asked the tinkling voice. "The clever boy had a backup plan. A rope at his ankle to stop his heedless rush for the water's embrace. Make a note sisters! The sailors are getting wiser." A moment later, I felt the light touch of her fingers on my ankle, but the blow to my head had briefly pushed the last sister's musical spell out of my mind.

I could feel it insinuating itself back into my ears, like a worm working itself into wet soil, but I pushed it back and shouted the first words of the greeting.

"Ladies numbered Three,

"Hearken unto me."

The fingers fell away from my ankle. I took a breath, gathering myself. I had more to say, and say correctly. If I was to have any hope at all.

"Rotting fish on a beach!" spat the beautiful one, her voice not so bright and tinkling. "He's started the incantation, sisters. Curses and carcasses. Now we'll be stuck bargaining with him."

"Be ye welcome on this ship,

I beg safe passage through the storm."

The last sister's ascending tone, so sweet a moment ago, became a roar, the bellow of a large beast gored, wounded but still dangerous. Then, all was silent again. The last sister was biding her time now. I knew this with sudden certainty. In the echo of her voice, still reverberating within me, I could feel her anger and frustration at being thwarted. It was like a hard grip on the back of my neck, tightening inexorably. How could I hear so much in her roar? *Truly, Mother, you were right. This last sister sang a song beyond language that cut right into a man's skull like a swung ax.*

I got slowly to my feet, aware that I was alarmingly close to the edge. The length of extra rope at my ankle, my lifeline that I was still tied to, lay black and loose on the deck like a dead snake.

The golden sister floated back over to the mast, her feet dangling a few inches above the deck. She made an impatient gesture for me to continue. Her lusciously full lips jutted out in a pout that somehow managed to make her more desirable. For all the world, she looked as if she was about to scold me for being naughty. She shook her head, a vision of disappointment, looking from me to the rope and back again.

"It's so much better if you don't resist," she complained. She raised an eyebrow when I didn't speak further. "Well, go on, complete the spell, boy. And we will bargain."

"Yes, I want something delicious from him," the hideous sister put in. "This fishy only whetted my appetite." She tossed all that remained of the dolphin, which was a piece of its tail, over the side. We listened together, but there was no accompanying splash. The ugly sister's eyes widened and she leveled her many-fanged smile on me. "Ah, our oldest sister has taken that morsel." She chuckled "No doubt, she'll want a piece of you, too."

"Mayhap," said the pretty one, drifting closer once more so I could smell her sweet flower perfume, "he's forgotten the rest of the rhyme. Wouldn't that be delightful?"

"Speak, boy!" shouted the giantess, "or I'll strip your flesh from your bone with relish!"

I opened my mouth. I knew the proper words of course. The words I had just said to Eben and he would expect me to say. The ones the Ladies, too, were waiting to hear. But I had other words my mother had given me, and these were what I uttered.

"Your hold on me, I do hereby strip,

I invoke blood tie, and break your charm."

Both the Ladies on deck stared at me in shock, their mouths hung open.

A sudden lurch beneath my feet almost toppled me. I fell against the nearby railing and gripped it hard as the ship listed first one way then the other. Wild with fright, I stared down at the dark boiling waters next to the ship. The surface parted like the curtains at a stage play. An immense shape rose slowly up, moving ponderously, deliberately, majestically, pushing the ship away from it with its sheer size. The last sister was finally showing herself. A wave of relief coursed through me. I needed all three to be present if I had any hope of fulfilling my purpose.

First, I only saw the crown of her black, hairless head, and then a face, somewhat like a person's, but without a nose, only a livid red mouth and two enormous green eyes, both as big as barrels. Instead of cheeks, two large flaps, big as a ship's sails, opened wide, then shut with a snap. She rose untold feet above me, her body seemed to nearly reach the very moon above. She was a dark pillar with evidence of a life lived under the sea all over her body; barnacles grew on her skin and skeins of seaweed clung to her sides. Peering down at me, the eyes sent beams of light out piercing the darkness. First one would blink and then the other. Never at the same time. Two long arms hung loosely at her sides, strangely flexible fingers twitched. I imagined her crawling on the ocean floor, the light of her eyes attracting fish into her open maw, as she bided her time, awaiting the next opportunity to join with her sisters on the surface above to take what they could from sailors. All the time, she waited for another chance to call sailors over the sides and into her arms.

If my mother had her way, this would be the last time she called.

This behemoth, this last sister, threw out an arm and grasped the side of the ship to prevent it from sliding further away. The ship shuddered as she drew it back to her. I saw close up she gripped with unnatural fingers, webbed like her smaller sister's, but three times as long and black instead of gray.

Her green eyes focused on me, one blinked, then the other, and then the great mouth opened.

"Did this mite dare to claim blood tie, sisters?" she asked.

I moaned. I couldn't help myself. Her voice was even more shocking than her awful appearance because it was the sound I had heard before, that had almost driven me off the ship, painful in its beauty, impossible to resist. It vibrated within me, the words she spoke echoing like I had a cave between my ears, empty of everything but the voice, the voice, the voice.

"He cowers before me," the last sister muttered like distant thunder, her voice thick with disdain. "He is no kin of ours."

I tried to speak but all that came out was a pained croaking. My mouth opened and closed uselessly, my tongue twitched, seemingly made of lead and just as flexible. Spittle leaked from between my lips and down my chin. My moaning grew louder, and I heard it distantly as if it came from someone else. My limbs suddenly without strength, I fell on my side and flopped about on the deck like a landed fish. All of this in a struggle to speak just a few words more. I had to utter the last couplet of the incantation if I had any hope of success. But at the critical moment, no words could come.

Oh mother help me now!

A golden glow neared me. I felt gentle fingers under my chin, and the beauty lifted my head. My twitching body stilled at her touch. She stared down at me.

"You have tied his tongue, dear sister. He wants to say more. Are you not curious about this supposed blood tie?"

I took a deep breath, hopeful, and my lungs filled with the noxious fumes of the swamp. The second ugly sister had neared as well.

"I say we eat him now," she said, her shadow looming over me, "and the sailors below too. We can do it, sister. After all, this whelp said the spell wrong and I'm awful hungry."

"You're always hungry, dear," said the beauty, "but this is the first curious thing to happen in hundreds of years. I want to know more."

A webbed hand, with a palm spanning my entire forearm, took hold of me, jerked me up a few feet to dangle like a puppet.

"I vote for eating. Think of all the delights below deck, sister. An entire ship of sailors, what soul-feasting you would have."

The beauty threw back her head and her tinkling laughter rang out like wind chimes in a sudden breeze. "'Tis true. I would delight in so many. And yet..."

Her eyes refocused on me. I could see she was tempted. At last, she looked out across the railing to the last sister.

"We'll make it a vote since we are tied. Our oldest sister will break it."

The ugly one dropped me back to the deck, and the two smaller Ladies stepped away and stared up at their sister. My eyes were riveted on her as well. What choice would she make? Was I to die here on this deck, my mission unfulfilled, the entire purpose for which I was raised washed away in an instant?

With her long, dark body towering over the ship, the oldest sister appeared to me like the dark pinnacle of some unholy temple. Her green lantern eyes regarded me with little more than contempt. Her eyes. Her green eyes. Like mine.

The only part of my body I had control of, at this moment, was my eyes. My mother's legacy. I willed them to stare up at the last sister and bend her to my will. I cast aside thoughts of her immensity, her power, her untold age. I opened my eyes so she could truly see me. I willed her to allow me to speak, to fulfill my destiny. One eye blinked at me, then the other.

Finally, the last sister said, "There is something..."

"There is!" said the beauty. "That's what I sense. His eyes..."

"I would grind them between my teeth!" shouted the ugly one, her frustration growing. "My dear sisters, hear me! This boy's words are some kind of trickery. I don't trust him and I don't want to hear more." She held up a clawed finger, the webbing stretching thin between her digits. "The one time – the one and only time, we changed the ritual, we paid. Do you not remember?

We paid. Lost one of our own." She pointed back at me. "This is a mere morsel. No kin of ours. Keep him in silence, dear sisters!"

The beauty tossed her golden mane and huffed. "I grow bored, if I'm being honest. Though I love you both. No, it's true! Don't shake your head at me, Hagatha! I've taken everything from the sailors I wish to, even their souls on occasion. I no longer have your hunger. I need more. Even a little diversion..." She turned her attention back to her oldest sister, the singing monster from the deep. "Hear me, Susra! A little diversion is all I need, all we need. Let us hear what this little morsel says. Blood tie? How could that be? It's probably nothing, but still. And if it's nothing then we eat him up, and the sailors too. Where's the harm?"

The ugly one, Hagatha, stomped a foot on the deck so hard the wood cracked. "Have you heard nothing I said? The last time - "

"Two days ago," interrupted Susra, "I ate a great whale. We had a battle that lasted two settings of the sun. I defeated her. Consumed her. And yet...I was not satisfied." She issued a rumbling sigh. "I agree with Tella. Hagatha, let us hear the child speak."

I felt the magical grip on me ease. I glanced down the length of my body, grateful beyond expression to see I still had the rope tied around my ankle. They had not thought to untie it, and if all went to plan I might need it again. I sat up, shaking the clouds from my vision.

I felt their eyes on me and looked up.

Hagatha had her arms crossed over her chest, scowling. Tella, the beauty, was smiling sweet and expectant, her eyes eager. Beyond them, Susra, the ancient one, blinked one eye, then the next.

"What would you say, child?" Susra said.

"Yes," Tella piped in. "Be quick. How can you invoke blood tie? Tell us before Hagatha scarfs you down in three bites!"

For her part, Hagatha only glowered, stewing in her anger.

A memory came to me, flashing through my mind like a lightning strike. My mother's hand on my shoulder, as she lay dying on her bed. Her own emerald eyes staring into mine, her face thin and waxen.

"For your father," she had said, "make them pay."

Gripped in her other hand was the strange dagger. She had passed it solemnly to me. It was a weapon from the deep sea, a handle made of coral and a blade made not of metal but of some hardened bone taken from a creature my mother knew from the time before - when she had not been human.

"Take it," she had said, choking for air, closing my fingers around its handle. "Poison to my sisters. The blade. One cut each. All it takes."

She had smiled at me one last time, then turned and looked out the window to her beloved garden. She took two more breaths, and was gone.

Now, nearly three years later, I sat on the deck staring up at her three sisters. The blade my mother had given me tied to my forearm with two knotted cords. I opened my mouth, about to speak, then abruptly leaned forward, as if I were about to be sick. At the same time I reached up my left arm sleeve. Two quick tugs at the knots, and the blade was free in my hand.

I looked up again. Tella had cocked her head to one side, suddenly suspicious.

I called out in a voice all three could hear:
"Ladies numbered Three,
Hearken unto me,
be ye welcome on this ship,
I beg safe passage through the storm,
Your hold on me, I do hereby strip,
I invoke blood tie, and break your charm..."
Watch over me now, Mother! I plunged on:

"My mother was your sister, when the Ladies numbered Four,

For my father's death at your hands I settle the score!"

"No!" screamed Tella. "It cannot be!" Her beautiful face ugly for once, a rictus of pain. As the glow of her skin dimmed, her feet sank to the deck.

I didn't wait for further reaction. I rushed forward, blade at the ready. Tella raised an arm to ward me off, squealing in panic. If I could only cut her once...

But my moment of surprise was gone.

In my periphery, I saw a blur of motion. Hagatha.

I lashed in that direction with the blade, felt the knife dig in somewhere, into something, and stick fast, heard a grunt, and then a bunched fist hit me in the head. I went airborne, sailing over the side of the ship leeward, clinging to consciousness only by a slim thread.

A jerk on my leg told me the blessed rope had held, and brought me back to full awareness. I banged against the side of the ship with a thump like a beat on a massive drum. Waters roiled beneath me, thirty feet below. I was dangling perhaps five feet over the edge.

My years of training, both under my mother's tutelage and the three years since her death before coming onboard this ship, put me in good stead. I swung up, gripped the rope, and hand over hand started to pull myself back to the deck. I had to get that knife back again.

Hagatha was howling in agony.

"Pull it out!" she shrieked. "It burns!"

"I'm trying. If you'll only hold still a moment," Tella told her sister. "Why, it's just a little knife. You get far worse hurts hunting sharks. Did he really think he could kill us with this?"

I got one leg over the railing and pulled myself back on deck.

"Susra!" Tella called out as she leaned over Hagatha's arm. They were only a few paces away from me. "Where's the boy? Did he fall in the water?"

My stomach sank as I heard the eldest sister say, "Behind you Tella. I'll hold him."

Susra started singing again. The double tones filled my skull, calling to me, ready to interpose their will.

And I almost laughed for joy. I was immune to her magic. As my mother had often said, completing the words as she instructed would free me of their magic, at least until the final hour was complete. Because Susra's singing spell didn't work on me, I must still have time and could resist their magic.

But I kept my laughter firmly in check. My mother had counseled me numerous times on succeeding should this moment ever come. One thing she had emphasized was that strength was necessary, yes, but even more important would be cunning.

With that in mind, I fell to the deck and began convulsing again. I even produced drool, as if Susra had bewitched me once again.

Tella laughed, delighted. "All this talk of revenge, and look at him. Pathetic! Our nephew could inflict but a single wound on Hagatha. Oh, how I wish Despera were here to see her son fail!"

Tella walked over to me, away from her wounded sister. "It is strange I cannot float. Ah well, let me eat his soul now. What a diversion this is! Come on over, Hagatha, and you can suck the marrow from his bones when I'm done. What a feast for both of us! Hag - ?"

Hagatha sank to the deck with a moan.

Susra's song cut off abruptly. "Sister!" she thundered.

Tella spun to her fallen sibling. "What's happened?"

The moment she turned, I sprang up and shot toward the fallen Lady. She lay on her back, her breath coming in short gasps, her complexion even grayer than before. I saw my mother's knife buried in her shoulder, up to the hilt, and made that my goal.

Tella made a grab at me, but without her gliding ability, I found I was just quick enough to elude her. Three more quick steps and I had the knife hilt in hand. I gave it a tug. It wouldn't come free.

Hagatha shrieked in pain, but her voice was weakening by the moment. She hit at me with her uninjured arm, but only managed to bat at me like an overgrown kitten.

"She's dying!" Tella cried in sudden alarm.

I knocked Hagatha's arm aside, got my legs under me as well as a solid grip on the hilt, ignoring the black ichor that had begun spilling out of the wound and out of Hagatha's mouth. I pulled with all my might. It gave a little. A little more. Almost there.

A shadow above me. I looked up in time to see Susra's massive webbed hand swinging down, trying to smash me into the deck. At this point, she seemed not to care what damage she did to her sister's dying body.

I fell backward, losing my grip on the knife. I was plunged into immediate and complete darkness, as though a giant ocean wave had crashed down on me. My first thought was that Susra had crushed the life out of me. But the wet membrane pressed onto my face and the feeling of wood at my back told me I still clung to life. I realized that my momentum and blind luck had carried me under the pliable webbing that spread between Susra's fingers. I had not been smashed, but was trapped.

I flung my arms and feet out wide underneath the slimy webbing, hoping that somehow I would knock a limb against the knife, get it back in hand and be able to wield it. I struggled for a moment and then went still. Susra had not yet lifted her hand.

I listened.

I could just make out the two living sisters' voices, but their words were muffled because of the layer of webbing.

Where is your knife, Mother? Let it be close.

Without warning, Susra pulled her hand away. Before I could scramble to my feet, Tella had me from behind by the shoulders in a grip every bit as strong as Hagatha's had once been. I looked around desperately, seeking the knife, but I didn't see it anywhere.

"You're finished, little nephew," Tella cooed in my ear as she lifted me to my feet. "Your weapon is nowhere to be found. Perhaps Despera would be proud to know you killed one of us. Perhaps. But in the end, you have failed. She has failed."

Tinkling laughter, a nibbling on my ear, a tousling of my hair.

"Now that I know your parentage, it all comes clear. Yes indeed, you are quite comely like your father. But Despera, dear sister – what a fool! She never should have forsaken us to become human. For what? She had to know we'd find him and steal him from her! Even though he'd given up sailing the sea, he should have gone as far away from it as possible. Susra searched for a few years, found him, and once she did, she called him off the edge of the lighthouse. Such a laugh we had at his ending. Well, we thought that was the end of it. And Despera would age and die without him. A fitting ending for her as well, without her lover. We never thought, though, that their union would result in you - a son."

Her grip was steel on my left shoulder, but she touched me lightly on the neck with her right hand. "Perhaps it is fate that brought you to us, my little diversion. Hagatha had grown tiresome of late. But now we have you. And we have a blood tie. We will need more sisters to join us. You, my little morsel, can be their father."

I jerked away from her touch and the tinkling of her

laughter sounded like glass shattering over and over.

"Susra!" Tella cried in triumph. "He doesn't seem to like my little idea."

We both looked out off the side of the ship to where the black column of Susra's body still stabbed up to the sky above. The green eyes blinked at us, first one, then the other. But she remained mute. I thought the light coming from the green lantern eyes looked weaker than they had before. Was it only my imagination?

Susra extended a hand toward us.

"Perhaps," Tella said, "Susra wants to just kill you. I'll defer to her wisdom. He's here sister, what say you? Kill him now, or keep him for stud?"

Susra remained silent, the hand drew near, hovered over us, the webbing between her fingers blocking the moon.

A drip of ichor hit my nose, falling like rain. More spots of it flecked the deck like a spray of black oil.

Susra massive hand shuddered and I saw the knife, my mother's blessed blade, fall with a thud to the floor below.

The knife had pierced and caught in Susra's finger when she tried to crush me.

"I die," Susra breathed out, in a voice like a thousand voices sighing.

The sea all around the ship foamed and her massive body began to sink beneath the depths. The hand above us drifted away. It clutched at the railing, caught it for a moment, making the ship tilt. I wondered if she would drag us all down with her. But in the end, her fingers slipped free and Susra was gone.

Through it all, Tella's grip never loosened, though her breathing came in frantic gasps.

"How could you?" she asked at last.

I kept my eyes on the dagger, lying there in the pool of Susra's black blood, a few feet away. Feet that felt like miles.

"You should have left my mother alone," I said.

Tella ignored that. "I suppose I can't possibly kill you now. No indeed. You will have to serve as my mate, for however long I need you. Much as I hate you. And once I have enough new sisters, I will kill you. Kill you slowly."

She moved around to face me, blocking my view of the dagger.

"Or maybe," she said with a smile, "I'll have our spawn kill you. Yes. I'll enjoy watching that happen. Who knows what children you and I can raise up from the deep?"

She stiffened and looked up at the sky. "The hour has ended." Her skin began to glow with its telltale golden hue. Her hands, gripping both my shoulders, warmed. "My power returns." She rose once again to float a few inches off the deck.

I felt the muscles of my body relax. I smelled the flowers of my mother's garden once again, so intense they could not be denied. Tella's green eyes bored into mine. "You're mine for as long as I want you, little morsel. My dear, dear nephew."

Over her shoulder, I saw a furtive movement. I had no idea what or who it could be, but I had sense enough not to react. I allowed myself to get lost further in Tella's eyes. I felt the grass under my feet. I saw Tella approaching me in a field of bobbing blossoms. Her hair was loose and spilled over me to tickle my nose. I would give her whatever she wanted. I would give her...

She screamed and I was at once back on the deck with her.

Her hands fell away from me and she fell onto her side. A second later, black ooze shot from her mouth, her nose. She rolled onto her stomach and revealed a knife wound in her back.

Standing before me, my mother's knife in his hand, stood Eben. He looked down at the dying Lady and then back at me.

His eyes were wide, brimming with tears.

"Eben," I cried. "How did you think to..." I looked down

at Tella's body.

"The hour was up, lad. I been waiting at the door, fearful about how you acted so strange afore I left, so when the captain said the sand was done, I came right out. I saw...I saw you with her. *Her.* One of them that took my leg all those years ago. The knife was just lying there, her back was turned, and I thought...I thought..."

"You thought right, Eben," I said. "Exactly right."

We looked back down at Tella, the last of the Sisters, the last of the Ladies Three, dying on the deck at our feet, her limbs losing their shape, the flesh turning quickly green then black, decomposing in mere moments. *I hope you're somehow seeing this, Mother. The reign of your sisters had ended, the loss of your love avenged.*

"I thank you," I told Eben. "My mother thanks you."

"Who are you, son?" he asked. "Tell me true. I heard her say 'nephew.'" He eyed me a moment as I hesitated, unsure what to say. I opened my mouth, closed it, opened it again. At last, he held up a hand to stop me. He passed the blade to me. "Maybe I don't want to know."

"What in God's name is this mess on my deck?" the captain's voice rang out. "Some sort of oil spill? Why are you two just standing there?" The captain stomped past us, hourglass in his left hand, his trusty whip in the other. "We survived the Ladies, and the boy looks none the worse for wear. To work, to work." He stalked out of earshot.

Eben winked at me. "Back to work on the Sea of Sorrows, lad. Back to work."

He limped off after the captain.

I smiled, relief and disbelief competing within me. Work? The real work was finally done. I lifted my chin, closed my eyes, and breathed in the sea air. Tasting the moment.

Rest well, Mother. Find peace.

Still smiling, I went looking for my mop and bucket. It was time to clean the last stain away.

The Annuity Squad

by James Kenneth Rogers

The doorbell rang.

Ralph Lund muted the Cardinals game he had on TV. He hadn't been paying attention anyway. Not today. All alone in his little place in the trailer park. Exactly one year since *it* had happened. A sort of anniversary. And now a visitor?

He set his beer down—a Sam Adams, at least, not a Bud Lite or a Natty Ice. He still had a little pride. Then he pushed himself up from the old recliner and opened the door.

He was surprised to see a beautiful young woman with jet-black hair standing in the late afternoon sun. She wore a nice, tailored suit jacket paired with a short skirt that revealed her shapely legs. The red lipstick on her lips glistened as she broke into a giant smile. She was with two men—one on each side of her. Each man wore a dark business suit and a giant smile. Behind them were a camera crew and some other hangers-on. The man on her left held a giant, blank rectangle of posterboard. The guy to her right was holding a big bunch of helium balloons of various colors. Someone in the group behind held a big cake.

"Ralph Lund?" the woman asked.

The cameraman was filming. The sound guy kept a microphone boom hovering overhead, just out of the camera's line of sight.

"Uh, yes?" Ralph said, his eyes narrowing. *Was this some kind of scam?* "And you are?"

"Well, my name is Abby Moore, and we're here to say," she paused.

"Say what?"

"Congratulations!!" she chirped. "We're with the National Publishers Company Prize Posse. You've won our sweepstakes!!"

The man to her right flipped around the posterboard. It was one of those giant novelty checks Ralph had seen on TV, but never in person. The amount written in the box had a lot of zeros —seven of them, to be exact. Ten million dollars. And right above the amount were written the words "Pay to the order of: Ralph Lund."

His mind flashed back to that time a few months back at work when Jack had pranked all the guys in the lottery pool. Jack had bought a new ticket with last week's winning numbers, and then slipped it into the lottery ticket pool for the previous week. There had been some pretty rowdy celebrations when the guys saw the fake ticket and thought they had all become millionaires. Jack finally fessed up when John Thomson said he was going to quit right away, and make sure to tell the boss what he really thought of him. Once they had gotten over the disappointment of not winning, they had had a good laugh about it, and joked about it for weeks. They had even renamed the lottery pool: "The Almost-Millionaires Club."

"Are you guys for real?" he asked.

Would the guys try to pull the same kind of prank on me again, and on today of all days?

"The guys at the warehouse didn't, like, put you up to this or something? I mean, I did tell a few of them I had entered the sweepstakes. . . ."

"We are completely serious," said the man holding the bouquet of balloons. He hadn't stopped smiling. "Would the guys at the warehouse have a Prize Posse van?" He pointed back to the curb, where a big white van sat parked with a big "Prize Posse" decal plastered on the side.

Ralph looked at the camera crew. They were still filming. Those cameras looked real. And there was no way the guys at the warehouse would have paid for all this just as a prank. And even for them, a prank like this would have been too much—on the one-year anniversary of his divorce. How would they have even known?

No, this was real.

Ralph let out a whoop. He pumped his fists several times, then grabbed onto the door frame to steady himself. He took a deep breath.

"OK, so what happens next?" he asked.

The following hour was a blur. They had him pose for pictures with the check. And with the balloons. And with the Prize Posse. Lots of those. That was his favorite part of it all. The Prize Posse girl—Abby—was always right next to him in every picture, brushing against his shoulder or posing with his arm around her waist. It was nice to be close to a beautiful woman. It had been a long time.

After the pictures, they interviewed him about what he was going to do with the money. He gave them a bunch of generic answers—buy a big house, and a boat, and a motorcycle, and a nice cabin in the woods. He didn't want to say anything embarrassing.

I'm going to pay off all that back child support so I can see my kids again. I'm lonely, and I miss my kids. And they need a father in their life. Yeah, that would sound great on national TV.

"OK, time for the cake," said a man who had been directing things and whom Ralph assumed to be the producer. "Is there anyone else we can film you celebrating with?"

"Uh, no, not really," Ralph said. "I live alone. Since the divorce, anyway. It's been exactly a year today."

"Oh, that's so sad," Abby cooed, rubbing his arm.

"Are there some neighbors you can invite over?" the producer asked. "You know, to make everything look more festive? We get a lot of good advertising out of these videos. There wouldn't be any sweepstakes if we couldn't sell our magazine subscriptions, you know."

"Uh, sorry, probably not," Ralph responded. "I mean, I *could*, but it'd probably be weird. I haven't lived here very long. I mean, we wave 'hi' when we see each other coming and going. But other than that, everyone pretty much keeps to themselves. You know how it is nowadays."

Deanna from down the street came out onto her tiny front porch to smoke a cigarette. She was a pretty brunette in her early thirties. It looked like she lived alone. Several times over the last year, Ralph had thought about trying to strike up a friendship with her—maybe even asking her out. But he always chickened out in the end.

He briefly considered inviting her to come over to join the celebration but ultimately decided against it.

Once Deanna was done with the cigarette, Ralph noticed she lingered outside, just watching. They filmed him cutting the cake and celebrating with some of the crew and the members of the Prize Posse. A few curious neighbors spied on the proceedings from their windows.

And then it was over. As the camera crew started packing up, a black SUV pulled up and parked on the narrow trailer park street, right behind the Prize Posse van.

"Now that we're done with the publicity part, Ralph, it's time for the actual business, so you can get paid," the producer said.

A man got out of the SUV and started walking toward them.

"You mean I can't just take that giant check to the bank and cash it?" Ralph joked.

The producer let out a forced laugh. "I'm afraid not."

A dog barked outside. Ralph looked out the window. An older couple were walking their dog—a mini schnauzer—down the narrow sidewalk. Ralph shook his head. After he fell behind on child support, the only visitation right the judge *hadn't* taken away was for the dog. Ralph still had the legal right to keep the dog every other week. He looked into his trailer at the calendar hanging on the small fridge. The next day—Monday—was highlighted in yellow.

Well, look at that, Ralph thought. *Tomorrow's supposed to be my day to pick up Burns.*

When Ralph had first moved in, he had carefully marked for the rest of the year each day when he was entitled to pick up his dog Burns for visitation rights.

What a waste of time all that calendar marking had been, Ralph thought.

When Ralph had tried to keep Burns at his place, it had been a disaster. Burns was an Airedale Terrier—a beautiful, loyal dog—but also a *big* dog. He just couldn't fit comfortably in Ralph's tiny place with a yard too small for a Chihuahua, much less Burns. That first week of Burns's visitation had also been his last. Ralph was sure his ex-wife's lawyer and the judge had colluded on that— letting him keep visitation rights over the only thing that could never work out in his little trailer.

Well, pretty soon, I'll have a house big enough for Burns to stay in. The kids and I will be able to play fetch in the backyard with him, just like we used to.

The man from the SUV had gotten up to what passed for Ralph's front porch—a square, four-by-four deck made of old, weathered wood that was shaded by a small, rickety awning. The new guy looked to be in his mid-forties. He was tall and had an athletic build. He had a crew cut, and his dark suit was clearly something that had come off the rack at a mid-tier department store. It somehow didn't fit him quite right.

"This gentleman," the producer said, motioning toward the man, "is the one in charge of ensuring you get paid. Ralph, I'd like to introduce you to Derek Hunter, head of our Annuity Squad."

"Annuity?" Ralph said. "What if I just want a lump-sum payment?"

A shocked expression crossed the producer's face. He quickly regained his composure, but not before Ralph noticed. The producer and Derek exchanged looks.

The producer opened an expensive-looking leather folder. He consulted a paper inside. "You're Ralph Lund, of 526 East Saguaro Lane, right?"

"That's me," Ralph said.

"All right, just wanted to make sure we've got the right guy before I leave you here with Derek," the producer said. "We, of course, like to know a little something about our contest winners before we show up. You know, to make sure you'll be at home when the Prize Posse arrives, that sort of thing." He looked down at his folder again. "It's not often, but sometimes our information can be wrong. For example, it says here that you're 67 years old, and that can't be right."

"No, no, you probably got your information mixed up with my dad, Ralph Lund Senior. I'm Junior."

"Oh, well that explains it, too bad, too bad," the producer said, shaking his head. He looked down at his paper again, "But you *are* a forklift driver at the warehouse for Wolfson Construction Supplies, right?"

"That's right," Ralph said. "Is there a problem?"

"No worries, you're still our winner! The name and address are definitely a match. You're the only Ralph Lund who would have entered the contest from this address, right?"

"Right, that's me. So why were you asking about my job

and all that?"

"Well, I was just surprised to hear you talking about annuities and lump-sum payments," the producer said. "Most contestants don't know what any of that financial mumbo-jumbo means. That's where Derek usually comes in." He pointed to Derek. "He's here to explain your . . . options. You know, that ten-million-dollar prize only actually adds up to ten million dollars if you take it as an annuity. Usually, we need to explain what all of that means. Help you pick out the annuity that makes the most sense for you."

"I know what an annuity is," Ralph said. "I'm pretty sure I can figure out for myself which option would be best. I used to be a CPA, you know."

"A CPA?" the producer asked, choking a little.

"Yeah, you know, a certified public accountant," Ralph said.

"Oh, how . . . *nice*," the producer said. His voice had the same tone he might have used if Ralph had said he had been a former drug dealer or porn movie director. "This is an . . . . unexpected development. Aren't you a little overqualified to be a forklift driver?"

Ralph leaned in and added quietly. "Got my CPA license yanked in the divorce. The accounting board said they had received 'credible evidence of criminal conduct' on my part. The ex was spreading all sorts of lies about me. Criminal stuff."

The producer was looking uncomfortable. Derek just stood there, impassively waiting.

"Don't worry, none of it's true," Ralph went on. "The police cleared me and everything. But the accounting board, well, they didn't care. Wouldn't even look at the police report fully exonerating me. Said I'd have to appeal the license revocation. Problem is, I can't afford a lawyer. I'm still trying to get my license back on my own. No luck so far."

"But you work at a warehouse now?" Derek asked.

"Those child support checks don't pay themselves." Ralph paused and shook his head. "Not that it matters, I guess. The judge set the child support payments based on my old CPA salary, which is three times what I make at the warehouse. I'm lucky if I can manage to pay half of what I owe each month." He sighed. "My kids deserve so much better than this, but it's the best I can do. The judge won't even let me see my kids until I'm all caught up on my payments. And the way things have been going, I have no prayer of catching up until my kids are both in their thirties. I tell you, this sweepstakes is going to really turn things around for me and my kids."

A sour look flashed across the producer's face.

"Hey, sorry, man," Ralph continued. "That was too much personal information, huh? I guess I'm a little too excited about this sweepstakes win."

The producer smiled. "No worries, we get the full spectrum of reactions. I've seen it all. How old are your kids?"

"The youngest is eleven, and the oldest is sixteen." Part of his mind told him to stop with that, but he went on anyway. "They need a father. This sweepstakes thing is going to be a real lifesaver for me, and for my kids."

"Well, it sounds like you have a lot to talk about with Derek," the producer said. "He'll tell you all about how you can get paid."

"That's right, sir," Derek said. He held out a hand, a serious expression on his face. "Like he said, my name is Derek Hunter, pleased to meet you."

Ralph shook his hand, noticing the strength behind his grip. "Nice to meet you."

"May I come inside?" Derek said. He held up a thick binder full of papers. "We do have a lot of paperwork to finish."

The camera crew had just finished loading their gear into

the Prize Posse van. Ralph watched wistfully as Abby climbed into the front passenger seat. "Are you sure Abby can't go over the paperwork with me instead?"

Derek let out a short chuckle and flashed a knowing look at Ralph. "You'd be surprised at how many men ask me that, but, no, I'm afraid it has to be me. Shall we?"

"Well, alright," Ralph said. "Come on in. We don't have far to go. It's only a single-wide."

He held the door open for Derek to enter the tiny kitchen/dining room. The walls were all covered in faux-wood paneling. The electric range was lime green. And the room smelled the same as always—sort of like a mix between an old car that had been left out in the sun too long, mixed with an old, musty basement, with just a hint of cigarette smoke left over from the prior occupants.

"Please, have a seat," Ralph said, motioning toward folding chairs and a collapsible card table that served as Ralph's kitchen table.

Derek sat on the folding chair on the opposite side of the table, positioning himself to see the front door and window. Ralph sat down on the only other chair, his back to the front door. This was the first guest Ralph had had in months. He was usually too embarrassed to invite anyone over. Not that he had many people to invite. Most of his pre-divorce friends had been "couple" friends of both him and Lauren—his ex-wife. And the wives in each of those couples had believed all the lies Lauren had told about him. They had all insisted that their husbands have nothing to do with that no-good deadbeat abusive Ralph.

"Well, this place is certainly . . . cozy," Derek said.

"Yeah, tell me about it," Ralph said. "And the location's great, too. Pretty bad crime rate all around here."

Derek looked around the trailer, as if taking in every detail. "I don't see an alarm system, though. I guess you wouldn't even need one."

"True," Ralph replied. "I don't have anything worth steal-ing."

"You'd certainly be able to afford an upgrade with your prize."

"Yes, the prize," Ralph said. "Let's hear it. What are my options?"

"OK," Derek said. The thick binder made a thump as he dropped it on the table. "I know this looks like a lot, but it's all just your basic, standard boilerplate legal mumbo jumbo. You know, giving us the right to use your name and likeness in our commercials. Providing your bank details for deposit—"

"Tell me more about the annuity and lump-sum options," Ralph interrupted. "What kind of interest rates are we talking about? What kind of repayment period? I sure could use a big in-fusion of cash *right now*, if you know what I mean."

"Yes, well, we at the National Publishers Company take the welfare of our prize winners *very* seriously."

Ralph rolled his eyes. He had spent enough years as a forensic accountant investigating and auditing companies accused of fraud that he had developed a keen sense for BS.

Sure, you care about prize winners, he thought. *You care about getting us on your commercials to show off the Prize Posse and get more magazine subscriptions.*

"We have several payout options you can choose from," Derek continued. He pulled a paper from his briefcase and slid it over to Ralph. "The option we recommend is the 'Triple Seven Plan.'"

"Triple Seven?" Ralph asked, raising an eyebrow. "Like, slot machines at a casino?"

Derek let out a dry, humorless chuckle. "No, nothing like that. What we've noticed is that a lot of our past winners tended to get . . . overexcited . . . by their winnings and spend it all right away. What's the point in becoming a millionaire, just to end up in the poor house a few years later?"

"And so your Triple Seven Plan somehow solves that problem?"

"Yes," Derek said, clearing his throat. "In a manner of speaking. It's a special 21-year annuity. The whole time, we give you a nice monthly payment of 9,920 dollars and 63 cents."

Ralph pulled up his financial calculator on his phone and punched in some numbers. "That works out to just 2.5 million dollars total. This is a *ten* million dollar sweepstakes, right? So, what happened to the other 7.5 million?"

"Yes, that's where the 'Triple Seven' kicks in. You see, the annuity is broken up into seven-year chunks. Every seven years, we give you a lump-sum payment of 2.5 million dollars. At the end of year seven, you get your first payment. Then again at years fourteen and twenty-one."

"And what other plans do you have?"

"That's the one we *really* encourage our winners to accept. You get a nice, guaranteed income for twenty-one years. That alone makes you solidly upper-middle-class. And it protects you from getting *too* much money at once, especially right at the beginning, when the thrill of winning can be a bit . . . overwhelming."

"Well, maybe I'm a bit of a thrill-seeker who likes getting overwhelmed."

"We discourage that. Studies show that prize winners—"

"I'm willing to take my chances. Doesn't the law *require* sweepstakes like yours to offer an option for a lump-sum payment?"

Derek's chiseled jaw clenched and moved side to side a few times. "Yes, that's right. We are *required* to offer a lump-sum payment. But, as you know, money now is worth more than it will be in the future. We are allowed to discount the lump sum by an appropriate interest rate."

"Oh yeah, sure, of course, I knew that. What's the interest rate they make you use?"

"State law here lets it be set at the discretion of the contest organizer."

"So, what do you do in states that mandate a certain rate?"

Derek's mouth made a grin, but his eyes remained mirthless. "We don't operate in those states. But not many states have a required rate. Most state legislators have realized that it's better to let businesses have the freedom to set their own rate. Land of the free, you know?"

"Oh, how . . . accommodating of all those state legislators. I guess you guys must have spent a lot on lobbying to get those laws passed." Ralph sighed. "Look, I already knew that lottery prizes end up being about half of what's advertised because of this trick. I was hoping I could get five million from you, just like the lottery, but I'm willing to take a haircut beyond that. I *really* could use some extra cash. I owe fifty grand in back child support. All my visitation rights have been canceled until I pay up. I miss my kids. And total, I'll need about another two hundred grand more to have enough to pay off all the rest until my kids turn eighteen. Not to mention hiring a good lawyer to fight this accounting board thing. Plus, I need to buy a house to get out of this," he held up his hands, "*cozy* place. Ten grand a month just isn't going to cut it. So, how much is the lump-sum payment?"

Derek scowled for just a second. He rifled through some papers. "Ah, here it is. This document describes our 'One-and-Done Plan.'" He slid the paper over to Ralph.

Ralph scanned over the paper. "This is a joke, right?"

"Mr. Lund, it's not a joke. This is a serious matter. Some of the best accountants and actuaries in the country worked to set that prize amount. It is very fair and reasonable, I assure you. The

One-and-Done payment is a lot of money."

"Just four hundred thousand dollars? That's it? *Four hundred thousand dollars?* This is unbelievable." Ralph punched some numbers into his calculator. "Your 'One and Done Plan' has a discount rate higher than 15 percent. That's the kind of interest rate a credit card company would charge. You're telling me with a straight face that this is a fair interest rate?"

"Well, I did tell you that we encourage our winners to choose the Triple Seven Plan. Why don't you choose that one? Now, there are two particularly important documents I need you to focus on," Derek grabbed the binder and started flipping through its pages. Once he found what he was looking for, he slid the binder back to Ralph. "This first document is information for prize inheritance. State law requires that your spouse have the right to inherit your prize. You mentioned that you are divorced?"

"That's right."

"Now, is that with a final divorce decree from a court, or are you just separated? These things make a difference. If you're just separated, your ex would still have the legal right to inherit—"

"No, we're really, fully divorced."

"Excellent, then please just check the box on the form saying so."

"What about my kids? Can they inherit? I'd like to leave something for—"

"I'm afraid not. State law, you know." Derek reached over to the binder and flipped to the next section. "This second document is our ten-page winners' agreement. On the last page, you'll need to sign and make your election. One-and-Done or Triple-Seven."

Ralph rubbed his forehead and flipped through the pages of the packet. *What kind of racket are these guys running here?* He thought. *The Triple-Sevens Plan will cost them more money. Why would they want me to accept it? And why is the One-and-*

Done only 400 grand? There must be some kind of angle. He looked Derek in the eyes. "Look, I think I need some time to think this over."

"Of course, of course. We think the decision should be obvious, but we understand if you need some time. Your first payment doesn't start until thirty days from now."

"*First* payment? You're just assuming I'll pick the Triple-Seven? But what if I pick the lump sum?"

"Oh, yes, of course. If you pick the lump sum, then it would be your *only* payment. I said 'first' because it's so rare for someone to pick the One-and-Done. In any case, payment is in thirty days, but prize election has to be completed within twenty-four hours." Derek looked at his watch. "It's seven p.m. now. Shall I come back tomorrow at six, and you can make your final choice?"

"Sure, that works. Tomorrow's a Monday, so I'll just be getting home from work."

"Very well, I'll leave the binder here. If you're having trouble sleeping tonight, feel free to read up. All that legalese will put you right to sleep."

"Thanks."

Derek stood. Ralph walked him to the door. Derek extended his hand. He had that same vice-grip again.

"See you tomorrow, Mr. Lund," Derek said.

Ralph stood in the doorway and watched Derek drive off along the narrow trailer park road. He went inside and poured himself a cup of coffee. He went back outside to his little porch, standing there and musing about his good fortune.

My life's finally turning around, he thought.

Deanna was still on her porch, watching. As soon as Derek was gone, she walked over. Her long brunette hair was up in a makeshift bun held together with a pen. She had on a yellow floral sundress that showed just the right amount of leg.

"Hey," she said shyly, looking at him with bright blue eyes. "I'm Deanna Kellis, from across the street? I introduced myself when you first moved in, but we haven't really talked since. Anyway, hey again.

"Hi," Ralph said. "Yeah, sorry about that. I've been meaning to. But, you know, I've got a lot going on right now . . . ." he let his voice trail off. "Do you want some coffee?" He held up his mug.

"This late in the day? No thanks. If I have caffeine after two, I can't sleep at night."

"Not me, I've got a fast metabolism. Even stuff like aspirin wears off fast for me. I can have a cup of coffee an hour before bed and sleep just fine. But with today's excitement, maybe I won't get to sleep anyway."

"Yeah, I couldn't help but see all the commotion. Did you just win the National Publishers Company sweepstakes?"

"Yeah." *Oh great,* he thought, *my neighborhood crush is a gold-digger.* "But you know, uh, they don't actually give you ten million dollars. They split it up into little payments over years. It's not like I'm an instant millionaire or something."

"Oh, I know. That's why I came over." She looked up and down the street. She leaned in, then started talking again in a more hushed voice. "That sweepstakes is bad news. I should know. My grandma won ten years ago." Deanna's eyes focused off into the distance. "She'd raised me since I was a kid. The Prize Posse came to our door, just like they did for you. TV cameras. Balloons. Cake. All of it. We were so excited. So much money! We were gonna move out of this trailer park." She motioned back at her trailer. "But here I am, still living in Gran's trailer."

"Your grandma's trailer?" Ralph said, looking over at Deanna's place. "But I thought you lived alone?"

"I do now, ever since Granddad and Gran died," she said. She blinked a few times and swallowed. "Gran picked the

National Publishers Company Triple-Seven plan. It was going to be so much more money that way. Even just the monthly payments were more money than we had ever seen. The checks came in, every month. Gran could even afford the payments for a nice brand new Cadillac." She took a deep breath. "But I tell you, that sweepstakes brought nothing but trouble. My granddad died of a heart attack just a few weeks after we won. Doctors said it must have been all the excitement from winning. But he'd never had heart problems before. And seven months later, Gran was gone too. She was driving to visit some cousins up in Payson. The police said she fell asleep at the wheel. Ran her car straight into the side of a mountain." She sniffled and wiped a tear from the corner of her eye. "And they say sevens are *good* luck," she added bitterly.

She sat down on the steps that led up to his little porch. After hesitating a moment, Ralph sat down next to her.

"So what are you trying to say?" he asked. "The Triple-Seven Plan is bad luck? It sure seems like a lot more money than the One-and-Done. Though, I have to say, getting a lot of money right away would certainly make my life easier."

"Nothing's gonna get easier if you deal with these guys." She looked up and down the street again. "Here's the thing. I've done some searches on the Internet. Well, not just some searches. *A lot.* The truth is, *nobody* ever survives long enough to get their big lump sum payment. They're dead within a year. Every single one—dead of a heart attack, an accident, cancer, usually stuff like that."

"You know, I always did think it was a bit odd that you only ever seem to see old people as winners in the commercials. So that's their racket, then? Only award the sweepstakes to old people, banking on them not surviving long enough to get their whole prize?" He looked over at Deanna, and remembering her grandparents, quickly added, "Though every death is a tragedy, of course. I'm not trying to minimize what happened to you. I'm just saying, maybe it's just that, what's happening is that old people die more often? I think they were expecting me to be an old guy too. It looks like they got me confused with my dad. I have the same name as him. I guess I lucked out. My gain is their loss." He laughed and leaned toward her a little and touched her elbow. "I guess you can be happy that the Prize Posse is gonna lose their bet on me this time. I'm young and healthy. I won't be dying anytime soon."

"Yeah, well, you got part of it right. It *is* usually old people." She folded her arms, as if shielding herself from a chill wind. "But it's not because they think old people will die sooner of natural causes. It's worse than that. Way worse." She shivered. "They kill them."

"So you're saying that all those old people who died of regular things that look like natural causes were really murdered?"

"It's not just old people." She unfolded her arms and looked into Ralph's eyes. "Every so often, someone younger wins. Probably because the company makes a mistake, like they did with you. I've only found three times where it happened in the last ten years. But get this." She grabbed his arm. "All three of those winners died the exact same way. Shot at night in a home invasion. And here's the thing. *Every* winner dies—the old ones, the young ones—it doesn't matter. And it's always in the first year. Usually right around the seven-month mark—I guess they figure by then, the publicity will have worn off, and no one will be paying attention."

"Are you serious?" Ralph said. He paused, then looked up and down the street. He leaned in and spoke in a hushed tone. "Well, tell me this—do you think these guys killed JFK too?"

She glared at him. "Look, this isn't a joke. Gran and Granddad are dead because of those bastards!"

He put his hands up. "OK, OK, I'm sorry, the Kennedy

joke was uncalled for. I'll admit, some of those guys from the Prize Posse do give off sketchy vibes. They're up to *something* shady. But killing prize winners? I don't know." He shook his head. "That seems like a stretch. Old people have been known to die of natural causes, you know."

"But *every* single prize winner? And all the young winners too? All dead in the first year?"

"Wouldn't someone have noticed by now?"

"C'mon!" She said, raising her voice. "Have you read a newspaper? Everyone knows most reporters are lazy, dishonest, or both." She hushed her voice again. "I've written to lots of reporters about this—anonymously. Shared all my evidence. And I've got lots of it. But they all ignore me. Maybe they think I'm just some nut on the Internet, or maybe they've been paid off. I don't know." She sighed and shook her head.

"OK, I get you on the lazy, corrupt reporter thing. But what about the police, though?"

"I took a chance on the local police and went in to talk to them in person. Figured I could trust them."

"And what did they say?"

She sighed again and shook her head, pulling a lighter and a pack of cigarettes out of a pocket in her sun dress.

"Do you mind if I smoke?" she asked.

"No, go ahead." He frowned a little.

She lit up and took a long drag. She turned away from Ralph and breathed the smoke out.

"I really should quit these things, I know," she said. "I just feel so stressed out all the time . . . anyway, the police. I showed a detective all my evidence. What he said was," she started talking in her best imitation of a gruff male detective voice, "'Maybe there could be a pattern here, but maybe it's just old folks dying of natural causes. You haven't given us any evidence of foul play.'"

"So they refused to investigate?"

"Yeah, they refused to investigate," she said, returning to her normal voice. She took another deep drag of the cigarette and let out the smoke, this time not bothering to turn. "They said that it was out of their jurisdiction since all the other deaths happened in other places. They told me to tell the FBI." She let out a mirthless laugh. "I bet you can imagine how well *that* went. They wouldn't even meet with me. Too busy looking for Russians under the bed, I guess."

"Well," Ralph said, trying to adopt a soft, non-confrontational tone. "You have to admit that maybe your story sounds a little far-fetched, right?"

"I swear it's all true." She put out the cigarette by grinding it into the stair she was sitting on. "I've tried so many times to warn prize winners. But there's a delay to the commercials. They usually only run months after the Prize Posse has been to someone's house. And they never tell you the person's last name either, so it takes some detective work to find them. I try my best, but every time so far, it's been too late when I found a winner's identity. They're already dead. And now, I lucked out, and they came right back to my street again. It must be fate." She laughed bitterly. "But the guy I'm warning won't listen."

"Well, do you have some proof?"

"I have an Internet site where I've cataloged every death. You can see for yourself. Go to SweepstakesDeaths.com. You haven't signed anything yet, have you?"

"Not yet. They're coming back tomorrow evening at six."

"Just be careful, OK?" Deanna said, her voice dripping with concern. She pulled the pen out of her bun and shook her head, letting her hair cascade down her shoulders. Ralph liked the way she looked with her hair down. Using the pen, she scribbled the website address on the palm of his hand. "Take a look at the site. Everything checks out. I promise. Just decline the prize and pray that they leave you alone."

Ralph rubbed his chin. This girl's theory sounded pretty out there. But she *was* really cute and seemed pretty normal otherwise. It had been a year since the divorce. Maybe it was time to put himself back out there. And reading her site might be a good way to have an excuse to see her again—and also figure out if she was crazy or not. "OK, I'll check it out," he finally said. "If you're right . . . well, to be honest, I hope you're not. I could really use the money."

"That's the thing," she explained. "Those Prize Posse folks always come around to neighborhoods like this. They know we're desperate and won't ask too many questions."

Ralph let out a heavy sigh. "Well, if you're right, I'm in big trouble. Maybe I should have just paid full price for those magazine subscriptions."

"I have a lot of news clippings about all the folks who got killed at home too," she said, motioning back toward her trailer. "If you want, well, maybe you could come over sometime tonight, and I could show you."

Over to her house? Already? Does this girl really just want to show me some articles? Maybe she is messed up in the head. "Uh, thanks, maybe I'll do that. Right now, let me read what you've got on your website. I want to see if there's anything to this."

"You better hurry," she said, brushing her hair out of her face. "You don't have much time."

She stood up. Ralph stood up too. They faced each other. Ralph realized they were standing just a little closer than two strangers usually would be. Her eyes were the perfect shade of blue.

"Well, Ralph," she said, extending her hand. "I'm glad we talked. Stay safe."

Ralph took her hand and shook it, feeling something electric as they touched. When they let go of each other's hands, she sucked in a deep breath and then took a half step back.

"Once you've seen my evidence, you'll know I'm right. Come on over, and I can show you more."

She turned and walked back to her trailer.

Ralph watched her. *How does she make that cheap sun dress look so good?* Then he shook his head. *Too bad she's crazy*, he thought.

Once inside, he got out his seven-year-old, beat-up laptop and set it on his kitchen table. As he typed SweepstakesDeaths.com into his browser, he noticed a grey sedan stop at the end of the street and park. No one got out.

That's weird, he thought. *I've never seen that car here before.* He stifled an urge to go spy on the car from his bedroom, where he'd have a better angle to see it. He shook his head. *Maybe her paranoia's contagious.*

He started reading her website.

* * *

Deanna had to be at work by nine a.m.

She had been up late, again, fiddling with the website and adding new case information. *Why did I stay up so late again?*

If she didn't leave within the next five minutes, she'd miss her bus, and she'd be late again. She was just grabbing a piece of toast to eat on her way to the bus stop when someone knocked on her door. She checked the peephole. It was Ralph.

She opened the door with her right hand and put her left hand on her hip. "I'm late for work."

"I looked at your site."

She looked at her watch. "And you want to talk about this *now?* You never came over yesterday. I would've had plenty of time to tell you all about it."

"Yeah, sorry about that. I spent time looking at your site. And checking the facts. I've got to hand it to you. Your site is well-done. Very convincing. I looked up as many cases as I could myself, and your stories checked out. All those people *did* win the sweepstakes. And they all really died."

"See? I told you! Are you going to refuse the prize?"

"Hey, I'm not saying you've totally convinced me. Maybe those old people really all just died of old age or real accidents. It would make sense."

"And what about the three young guys who died?"

Before Ralph could answer, she held up her hand. "You know what? Never mind, Don't answer. I don't have time. I've got to get to the bus stop to get to work."

Ralph looked down at his watch. "It's only eight o'clock. How long of a drive is it to your work?"

"Fifteen minutes, but the bus ride adds an extra fifteen, if it's not late. And it's *always* late."

"Well, fine then. You still have time to talk. I'll give you a ride." He pointed back toward the van parked in the carport of his trailer. "It's a 2009 Chrysler Town and Country with 193,000 miles on it. Yeah, it's a piece-of-junk old minivan, but that's what I got in the divorce, and I can't afford to get something else. It still runs, at least. I can get you to work, no problem." He looked up and down the street. His gaze lingered just a bit longer on a grey car parked at the end of it. "Look, I've got to tell *someone* about my plan. I called in sick today at the warehouse. I've got time to drive you. I need all day today to make some . . . arrangements."

She glared at him to make sure he knew she was still mad about him standing her up the day before. "Well, ok." Deanna stepped back and opened the door wider. "Alright, come in. But we gotta leave in twenty minutes. OK?"

Ralph nodded. He followed her into the kitchen. She had a small square wooden table with seats for four. She offered him a seat next to hers.

"Nice place you got here," Ralph said, looking around. "Bigger kitchen than mine. Newer trailer too."

"Well, granny managed to get us an upgrade to a double wide—before the accident." She finished the rest of the toast that had been in her hand. "Coffee?" She asked as she topped up her cup from a carafe sitting on the table.

"Sure, thanks."

She got a mug out of the cupboard and filled it.

"Like I was saying," she said. "If you think it might be just deaths from old age, then how do you explain the three young guys who died?"

"Those sweepstakes winners always come from poor neighborhoods. Like, well, you know." He pointed out to their street. "Maybe those guys just had bad luck. Three guys killed over the space of ten years. That could happen. I mean, why would a sweepstakes company just be killing people? But you're right, it does look suspicious. I'd say, right now, I'd give it fifty-fifty odds. *Maybe* you're on to something, but I don't know. . . "

"Well, you've seen all the evidence on my site, right? And I've got plenty more. Hard copies of newspaper articles. Coroner's reports. Death certificates. All sorts of stuff. But, you didn't come over. And now, I've got to get to work."

"I'm not sure your evidence matters, anyway."

"Huh?"

"I've got a plan," Ralph said as he smiled crookedly. "I'm going to take the money. And keep it. And not die."

"What!" Deanna said. "Well, then, you're a fool. Didn't you just say you thought it was fifty-fifty? That means a fifty-fifty chance of *getting killed.*"

"Yeah, yeah, I know," Ralph said, waving his hand. "But I've thought it all out. See, even four hundred grand could change my life. I could see my kids again. Move out of this dumpy neighborhood—"

"Hey! This is my *home.* Gran raised me here."

"But wouldn't you move out if you could afford to?"

"Well, yeah, I guess," she admitted.

"Like I was saying, I could move out. Maybe could afford a good lawyer to help get my CPA license back. *I could get my life back.* At least a lot of it."

"Get your life back? Yeah, except the National Publishers Company will take it from you anyway. Literally." She paused and shook her head. "I tried with you, I really did. If you want to be a fool and get killed, then I guess go right ahead."

"Hold on, hold on," Ralph said, putting his hands up. "I'm not going to die. I've got it all figured out."

Deanna raised an eyebrow. "You think so, huh?"

"Yeah, here's my plan," he said. "Let's say you're right. That they kill you before you can wait the seven years to collect your first big annuity payment. Well, then the key is to be prepared and make sure they can't kill you."

"So . . . your big plan is that you're not gonna let them kill you?" she asked. "Brilliant. And how do you do that?"

"Well, if they are killing winners, the problem is knowing *when* they're going to do it. You can't be on guard for seven months or a year straight. Even if you know they're after you, how are you going to keep watching for that long? You can't. So, you've got to force them to act on *your* timetable, when you want them to."

"Oh, I see. You're just going to schedule with their hit-men ahead of time? Set a convenient date?"

"Sort of," Ralph said. "The key is not being too greedy. That's how they beat you. Everyone takes the Triple-Seven plan because it's so much more money. But then the Prize Posse has months—or years—to kill you when you're not expecting it. So, the trick is, you don't wait. You take the lump sum. The One-and-Done. Then, they have to pay you within thirty days. Thirty days is a lot less time to watch out for them. Then you *know* when they'll be coming."

"And how are you gonna stay on guard and keep them from killing you, even for thirty days? Are you some kind of Special Forces guy or something? I thought you said you used to be an accountant. Is there some martial art for killing people with calculators and tax forms?"

Ralph laughed. "Funny. No wonder you're in your thirties and still single."

Deanna felt her face flush red with anger. "Hey! That was uncalled for. I'll have you know—"

He put his hands up in mock defense. "I'm only joking. You've had a lot going on in your life over the last ten years, and I can't imagine how hard the death of your grandparents must have been. You've been very resilient to come through all of that and figure out everything that you have." He lightly touched her forearm, which was resting on the table near him. "And by the way, yes, all accountants *do* get trained in martial arts. It's called 'Tax Kwan Do.' Did you know there are seventeen different ways to kill a man using only a calculator, a 1040 tax form, and a paperclip?"

Deanna laughed.

"Sorry if I'm being a bit loopy," Ralph said. "I haven't been this excited in years. I've got it all figured out!" His voice sounded excited, but Deanna could see a hint of fear in his eyes and tension in his forehead. "Maybe the killing thing is all wrong. In which case, I get four hundred grand with no trouble. But if you're right, I'll beat them by *not* fighting them." He drew his hand back and took a sip of coffee. Deanna was a little disappointed. She was starting to like him. "I don't need to. I just need to *avoid* them. Once the thirty days are up, they have to pay. If I can hide for thirty days, then I'll get my One-and-Done payment, and it'll be . . . *done*. I'll have my money, and they'll have no more reason to kill me."

"So your plan is to run away?" she asked. "Stunning and

brave of you. And how are you going to hide? Going to go to Mexico or something? You don't think they'll find you?"

Ralph scoffed. "Mexico? With all the cartel violence? No way. My life would probably be in more danger down there than it would up here with the Prize Posse. No. . . . I'm going camping for a month."

Deanna laughed. "This just keeps getting better and better. That's your big plan? To go camping for a month?"

"All I've got to do is lay low for a month. Out in the boonies, there's no traffic cameras to record your license plates. No cell phone towers to track your position. I thought you'd be impressed. Just look at how paranoid I'm being!"

"And what if they follow you out into the boonies and just kill you there? No one will ever find your body."

A look of dark intensity crossed Ralph's face. He looked out the window down the street. "I have that all taken care of." He was talking louder now, and slower, as if he wanted her to understand every word. "I have the perfect spot. A place my family's been camping for decades. It's on private property. Fenced off. Locked gate. It's on top of a ridge that'll let me see anyone approaching. And the few locals that do live around there? Well, they know *me*, but let's just say they don't like strangers." He leaned in close to her ear and whispered, barely audibly. "And I've got a Plan B too."

"Well, now you're sounding more paranoid than me."

He leaned back. "Maybe you're not as paranoid as you should be. Aren't you worried about putting all your research online? If they are killing people, isn't that dangerous for you?"

"I took precautions. I spent a *lot* of time educating myself about how. Like, I use a VPN—you know, a Virtual Private Network—it hides your location on the Internet. Plus, my website is registered anonymously. But to be honest, no one seems to care about what I have to say anyway. I've tried posting anonymously on social media sites. Reddit. Twitter. Places like that. It's hard to get noticed online."

"Well, you've got to go viral."

"Oh, is that all? It's that easy, huh?" She paused. "There was one time about three months ago that I started getting some attention. A Twitter post that some conspiracy theorists started sharing. People started checking out my site. Then, Twitter deleted my account, and the hits all dried up."

"Well, keep on trying, maybe it'll happen again," he said with a loud, cheery voice, but his face looked even more worried. He leaned in close again and whispered, barely audible again. "Now I *really* think some of your paranoia is rubbing off on me. Don't you think it's a pretty big coincidence the Prize Posse showed up to award a prize on your street three months after your site started getting a lot of hits?" He leaned back and said more loudly. "Say, could I get some more coffee?"

Her eyes widened. "Of course," she said loudly, pouring him more. She leaned in and whispered, "Why are we whispering?"

"Thanks for the coffee," he said loudly. He put his mouth by her ear and whispered, "I saw a strange car park down the street yesterday, just after you left. I can't tell if there's anyone in it, though, and I don't want to get too close to check and tip them off, just in case it's . . . something. Been there all night. If they *are* after me—or you—maybe they're listening in somehow, you know?"

Deanna looked at her watch. "We gotta go. Time for work." She leaned in and whispered, "Ralph, what are you getting into?"

"Ok, let's go," Ralph said. He leaned in and whispered, "I bet it's your fault. They probably picked me because I'm on your street."

* * *

They made their way to the van. Ralph half expected the strange grey car to pull out and follow them, but it didn't.

She leaned over so she could whisper to Ralph. "So that's the car you saw parked?" she asked. "Aren't you worried they might do something while we're gone?"

"No," Ralph whispered back. "I've got a doorbell camera. And I've made sure it points toward your house too. I've set it up to send out motion alerts. Anytime something moves in front of my house, or yours, we'll know."

He drove her to work with the radio turned up loud. He checked his rearview mirror more than a 16-year-old taking his driving test. He and Deanna kept up a loud conversation of inane small talk. But in between, they whispered, and planned.

As soon as Ralph dropped her off, he went to the sporting goods store—the only one that still sold ammunition.

He bought as much camping equipment as he could afford, which wasn't much. And when he was sure no one was looking, he surreptitiously slipped a few boxes of 9mm rounds into his shopping cart, hiding them under his other camping supplies. He absentmindedly patted his left pocket, where his modified Glock 43 was concealed in a pocket holster. It had only been six months since he had resolved all his court problems and gotten his gun back. There had been so much going on in his life, though, that he hadn't taken it to the range since then. But it would have to do.

As he pulled out of the parking lot, he carefully checked his rearview mirrors to see if he was being followed. He didn't see anyone, but how could he be sure?

He drove to the warehouse to say goodbye to the guys he worked with. It was 11 o'clock, the perfect time to see them and not have to worry about getting caught by any of the bosses for playing hooky from work. This was the designated time for smoke breaks. Most of the guys didn't smoke, but since it meant an extra 15 minutes of break time, they all pretended they did. All the guys would be out front, and none of the bosses would be.

Talking to the guys at work was his only social outlet these days. They were all rough, blue-collar sorts, but in many ways, Ralph liked them a lot more than his prior colleagues from when he worked as a CPA. These guys weren't afraid to tell you what they really thought. No PC garbage. No backstabbing office politics. Just lots of good-natured ribbing and the occasional hilarious prank. Ralph was going to miss them.

Too bad I'm not going to get the full 10 million, Ralph thought. *Then, maybe I could have bought Wolfson Construction Supplies and kept working here—as president.*

"Ralph, what are you doin' here?" Jack said. "You don't look so sick to me. What are you tryin' to pull on us? We had to yank Nate LaBenz in from inventory to sub for you on the forklift. And you know how slow he drives that thing."

"Hey!" Nate said. "You think I'm slow, huh? That's not what your sister told me last night."

The guys all laughed.

"Sister?" Jack said. "I don't *have* any sisters. Are you sure it was a girl you were out with?"

"Well, maybe your mom—"

"Hey, guys, I don't have much time," Ralph interrupted.

"You too busy being sick, huh?" Jack asked.

"Yeah, sorry about that," Ralph said. "But this *is* the first time I've ever called in, you know. I just wanted to let you know I'll probably be quitting. I may have come into some money, and I can't be. . . well, it's probably best that I don't tell you exactly what's going on. But I probably won't be coming back here to work."

"What, you get all your legal problems fixed?" Jack asked.

"Something like that."

"That's great!"

A few guys high-fived Ralph.

"Well, and since I may not be working here anymore, I wanted to say, well," Ralph choked up a little. He swallowed. "You guys are the smelliest, laziest guys I've ever worked with."

They all laughed.

"No, seriously, thanks, guys. You all helped me stay sane through some pretty tough times. I'm going to text you all a website later today. Please read it if you ever wonder what happened to me. Like about my life. It'll explain a lot."

"A *website*?" Jack said. "That explains stuff? About what? About life? Did you go off and become a Mormon or something?"

"It's not Amway, is it?" Nate asked.

Ralph laughed. "No, no, nothing like that. You'll see."

After leaving the warehouse, Ralph went out to eat for the first time in six months. He took his time enjoying a nice steak and a baked potato. It was two o'clock when he finished. He wanted to savor the meal, but it wasn't just that. He had been dreading the next step in his plan. Once he knew he couldn't delay any longer, he finally got up from the table.

He drove to his ex's house—what had been *his* house. Parking the car, he scanned the area carefully. There were no other cars in the cul-de-sac or on the connecting street. It didn't look like anyone was following him.

He got out and looked at the house. The one they had picked out so many years ago as the perfect place to raise a family. Nice quiet neighborhood. A big yard where the kids could play. He sighed, got out of the car, and walked up to the door. The yard still felt like home, but also, now, not-like-home. Lauren had torn out the rose bushes. And there was one of those "In This House . . . " yard signs out front.

He knocked.

A few seconds later, Lauren opened the door. Her dyed

blond hair was pulled back in a ponytail. She looked a few pounds heavier since he had last seen her, and she was wearing an old baggy Nike t-shirt. The one he had always hated. "What are *you* doing here?"

"I'm here to pick up Burns. It's my week, remember?"

"Really? Just out of the blue, you want the dog? You haven't taken him in months. I bet he doesn't even recognize you."

Just then, Burns came into the house from the backyard through the doggy door on the back wall of the family room, the one that Ralph had spent a whole weekend installing.

The shaggy black and tan dog let out a happy bark and wagged his tail excitedly. He ran to Ralph and jumped up, resting his front paws on Ralph's waist, standing on his hind legs so his head came up to Ralph's chest. Ralph stumbled back a half-step—Burns was two feet tall at his shoulders and weighed 100 pounds.

"How are you doing, Burnsie?" Ralph said happily, petting Burns' head while Burns eagerly licked Ralph's face. Ralph inspected Burns's shaggy black and tan fur. "Look at how long your fur is! Someone hasn't been getting you groomed." He scratched Burns' back. I've missed you, boy." Ralph looked up at Lauren, smirking a little. "Looks like he still recognizes me."

"Ralph, you can't just show up whenever you want like this. The kids will be home from school soon."

"They've still got an hour till school gets out. Don't worry, I remember. I'm not allowed to see them until I pay up. Kinda hard to do without my CPA license, you know."

"That's not *my* fault, I—"

"Yes, it is, and you know it," Ralph paused and took a deep breath. Burns hopped down but kept wagging his tail excitedly. "Look, we don't need to argue about this. The judge said I get Burns every other week. My little trailer hasn't been big enough for him, but, now, well—"

"Did you move somewhere bigger, Ralph? How could you afford that? You know there's a limit on how much you can spend on rent. You're not allowed to spend more than—"

"I haven't moved, Lauren. I've just, sort of, figured out how to make it work at my place with Burns."

"Ralph—"

"Look, Lauren, it's my week. It's my right. Come on, Burnsie."

Ralph turned and walked back to his minivan. Burns excitedly followed.

"Ralph!" Lauren called behind him.

"Don't worry, I'll have him back on time," Ralph said over his shoulder as he walked away. He loaded Burns in the side door of the minivan.

Ralph was frustrated from having to see his old house and Lauren, and he was nervous about what was coming that night. He drove around for a while, listening to the radio to calm down. It was four o'clock when he pulled into the trailer park.

Two hours until Derek shows up, he thought. *That should be enough time to get ready.*

He turned onto his street. The same mysterious grey sedan was still parked at the end.

Ralph parked in front of his place. He went around to the back of his minivan and unloaded the stuff he had bought at the sporting goods store. He put one box of the 9mm ammo in his right pocket. Better to keep that close.

The first thing to do once I'm inside is to load the Glock, he thought.

As he started to shut the tailgate, Burns barked.

"Don't worry, Burnsie. I just need to carry this stuff inside, and then I'll get you. I can't have you running around the neighborhood while I'm unloading."

He set his stuff down and was about to head out to get

Burns when he heard a knock at his door. Ralph checked the peephole. It was Derek.

Ralph opened the door. Derek stood there, no suit this time—just khakis and a polo shirt. He was holding a briefcase. And now Ralph could tell why Derek's suit hadn't fit very well. His muscles were huge.

"Good afternoon, Mr. Lund," Derek said with a curt nod.

"Uh, hi, you're, uh, early," Ralph looked at his watch. "It's only 4:07. How'd you even know I'd be home?"

Derek grinned wryly. "Call it a hunch. You're playing hooky from work. Called in sick. Am I right? That happens a lot. Most winners do that. Who wants to clock in, when you've got millions on the way?"

"Thousands, you mean. The annuity payments, remember?"

"Well, it all adds up over time. May I come in, and we can get those papers signed?"

Ralph hesitated. He hadn't had time to get anything ready. His Glock was in his pocket holster, unloaded.

What's he up to? Ralph thought. *Why is he here early? They wouldn't try anything in broad daylight, would they? The young guys always get killed during a home invasion, at night. There'd be too many witnesses right now. And I've got to let him in so I can sign that paper to get my payout.*

"Sure, come on in." Ralph stepped back and motioned for Derek to enter.

Derek came in and sat down at the table. "So, have you made your decision?"

"Sure did." Ralph grabbed the binder off the counter. He had spent enough time poring over everything the previous night that he knew exactly which page to flip to. "All I need to do is sign, and then you witness it, and we're done, right?"

"Correct," Derek said, pulling out a pen.

Ralph checked the box on the form, signed, and slid the binder over to Derek.

Derek leaned forward and looked at the form. "Oooo, Ralph. I wish you hadn't done that. You made the wrong choice."

Ralph started to stand up. "Well, it was my choice to make, and I don't mean to be rude, but I have a lot to do right now, so now that we've signed—"

Derek stood up too. A reassuring smile was painted on his lips, but there was a steely look in his eyes. "Sure, I bet you have a lot to do right now." He put his hands in his pockets and shrugged.

Ralph peered out the window, looking for Derek's car. He was eager to get him out of the house as soon as possible. "Hey, where's your car? The street's empty. Yesterday you had a black—"

Before Ralph knew what was happening, Derek pulled his right hand out of his pocket. A gun was in his hand.

It made almost no noise as Derek fired it into Ralph's chest. Ralph felt a pain stab through him. He looked down to see the wound, but there was no blood. There was just a tiny silver dart sticking out. Ralph pulled it, wincing.

"Too late," Derek said, looking out the window. "It injects instantly."

Stunned, Ralph watched Derek close the mini-blinds at the window. Then the panic kicked in, and he began to run for the door, but only made it two steps before he tripped and toppled onto the floor. His legs just didn't want to work anymore.

"Yeah, another bad choice, Ralph," Derek said. "You should've stayed put. That's probably going to leave a bruise. But, I guess bruising won't matter much for you soon, anyway. That dart has a powerful muscle relaxant. Very specially selected. Powerful, but with a short half-life. It'll keep you paralyzed for, oh, probably seven hours. In ten hours, it'll be totally out of your system. Won't show up on any toxicology report." Derek pulled something out of his pockets. "But just in case, I've got these zip ties. We always have a backup plan."

Derek bent over Ralph and swiftly rolled him onto his stomach. Ralph tried to resist. He *willed* his body to react. To fight back. But he couldn't. His muscles just didn't work. Derek zip-tied Ralph's wrists behind him and then zip-tied his ankles together.

"Since you can't move," Derek said coolly, "we don't have to worry about ligature marks from you struggling against the zip ties, until we're done here."

Derek stood up and took a step back to look at Ralph.

"If you were onto us, why did you sign, Ralph?" Derek's voice was laced with disappointment. "We got our footage of you with the check and the Prize Posse. We had what we needed for our next commercial. If you hadn't signed, we wouldn't have needed to take things this far. There would have been no annuity or payout for us to cancel."

Ralph tried to respond, but only moans escaped his lips.

Derek flipped Ralph over onto his side. "Just in case you throw up. Gotta have you on your side. We can't have you aspirating your own vomit. *That* would raise questions on the autopsy."

Ralph tried to talk, but again, managed only moans.

"You thought you were being smart, didn't you?" Derek snarled. "Whispering to the girl, thinking we wouldn't hear you. Well, yeah, we couldn't hear what you were saying, but we knew you were up to *something*. And your little camping trip? Not bad for an amateur, but we saw right through that. It was a red herring, to force our hand. Leaving tomorrow, going camping where we couldn't get you. All to make us act tonight, so you'd know when we were coming and could be ready for us. Well, we were ready for *you*."

A knock came from the back door of the trailer.

"But you weren't expecting us so soon, were you?" Derek said as he stood up. "The Annuity Squad has a one-hundred percent success rate. We weren't about to let *you* ruin that for *us*."

Ralph heard Derek walk into the back room. He heard the back door open, but he was facing away and couldn't see who was coming in.

"All clear?" a woman's voice inquired. Ralph recognized the voice, but couldn't place it.

Footsteps clicked against the hollow trailer flooring. Ralph heard someone walk up behind him. A woman's foot stepped over him. A Doc Martens boot planted itself on the ground in front of him. Then came the other foot. Ralph realized that he could still move his eyes. He followed the boots up. The newcomer had jet-black hair and a stunning face with perfect makeup. It was Abby Moore from the Prize Posse. She was wearing a nice pantsuit—professional-looking, but something that allowed for a full range of motion.

She set a large handbag on the ground, then squatted down and looked into Ralph's eyes. "Hi there." She rubbed his arm, the same way she had yesterday. "Too bad you signed, Ralph. I actually liked you. I'd been hoping it wouldn't come to this."

She stood back up and turned to Derek. "Any sign of her?"

Derek walked to the window and peeked out of the blinds. "Not yet. Ralph, when is your girlfriend going to come over?"

Ralph moaned again.

"Don't try to answer, man. That was a rhetorical question."

* * *

Ralph's body was turned so he could just barely see the

microwave clock on the kitchen countertop. That was how he knew two hours had passed. Derek and Abby had left him paralyzed on the floor while they waited. Ralph's drool had made a wet spot on the carpet below his mouth.

Abby and Derek took turns watching out the front window. Every so often, they would call in status reports on their cell phones. Ralph tried to listen for clues in their conversations but couldn't deduce much. They used code language and lots of incomprehensible acronyms. It at least seemed clear that Derek and Abby were the only people here on-site. Whoever else they were talking to seemed to be back at "HQ" in Grand Rapids.

Sensation was gradually returning to Ralph's muscles. He felt the tingles and needle-prick sensation you get with a sleeping limb, but over his whole body. And, luckily, he could swallow again. He tried moving his legs. He was able to bend his knees, ever-so-slightly. There seemed to be a lag, though, like his muscles were working in slow motion.

Can I move again? He wanted to test things further but didn't want to make any movements that would draw Derek and Abby's attention.

He tried wiggling his fingers and found he could move them freely.

But hadn't Derek said the drug would last for seven hours? Does my abnormal metabolism strike again? Ralph said a silent prayer.

"She's coming over," Abby called to Derek from the window.

Deanna—no! Ralph thought. *Don't come in here. Run!* He tried to yell out a warning, but it caught in his dry throat.

"Finally," Derek said. He looked at his wristwatch. "It's 6:37. She made us wait long enough." He went to the door, and Abby positioned herself to the side of it. She was kneeling, holding a dart gun just like Derek's. It was aimed at the door, ready to fire as soon as it opened.

"Ralph?" called Deanna's muffled voice from outside. "Are you in there? I've been keeping an eye on things since I got home from work. I haven't seen anyone from National Publishers Company Prize come by yet. Did you cancel with them? I sure hope you did! Hello? Ralph?"

Derek looked through the peephole. "Damn. She's about six feet back from the door," he said quietly to Abby. "A little too far to grab quickly. But the street looks clear. On three, I'll open, you shoot, and I'll pull her in as fast as I can." Derek held up his hand in a fist. He held one finger up. "One."

"Ralph? Are you in there?"

"Two."

"Ralph?"

"Three."

Derek whipped open the door. Deanna screamed. Ralph watched, powerless. He saw through the open doorway as Deanna jumped back. Abby fired. The dart zipped past where Deanna had been. Deanna started running. Derek bolted out after her. Ralph heard Deanna scream, but then it was cut short. Derek carried her back inside. One of his massive arms was wrapped around Deanna's waist, holding her off the ground. He had his other hand over her mouth to keep her from screaming. Deanna kicked and struggled, but it was no contest. Derek was just so much bigger and stronger. As soon as they were inside, Abby slammed the door shut, and Derek threw Deanna on the floor beside Ralph. She landed on her back with a cry. She looked over at Ralph, and he saw her eyes wide with terror. Derek stood over her, quickly bringing his knee down on her stomach to hold her down.

"Get the zip ties!" he shouted to Abby.

Deanna fumbled around in her pocket. She pulled out something pink that looked like a futuristic ray gun. Just as Derek reached for it, she shot it at him. Two wires flew out of it and hit Derek in the stomach as the device made a crackling noise.

Derek stopped moving. His eyes rolled up, and his body shook. Then, he went back to normal. He started laughing, leaning harder on his knee and putting more weight on Deanna's stomach.

"A Taser? Nice try. But those don't even work half the time, you know. They're supposed to shoot barbs into your skin, then zap your muscles so you can't move. But the barbs you shot at me didn't even make it through my clothes. Just stuck in my shirt." He pulled the barbs out of his shirt. He grabbed the Taser out of her hand. "But you know what *does* work on these things? The electric shock mode. Basically, just turns it into a cattle prod."

"Dumb trailer park trash," Abby muttered.

Derek pressed the Taser into Deanna's side and zapped her. She screamed. He threw the Taser down, then flipped Deanna onto her stomach. He kept her pinned on the ground while Abby zip-tied her wrists and ankles.

While that went on, Ralph noticed that the tingling was abating. He felt like himself again.

Derek stood up and looked at Abby. "Someone might've seen something. We may need to get out of here."

Abby had her phone to her ear. She put her hand over the microphone. "HQ is checking police scanners and 911 reports. So far, nothing."

Derek rolled Deanna onto her side so she was facing away from Ralph. She was just a foot away from him. When Derek and Abby weren't looking at him, Ralph moved his legs and arms. No lag. His muscles seemed to work!

Derek kneeled in front of Deanna.

"You've got a choice to make, Deanna," Derek said. "We need the passwords to your website. Can't risk that thing going viral again."

"Website, what website?" Deanna asked.

"SweepstakesDeaths.com, does it ring a bell?" Derek said. "Come on. The play-dumb act isn't going to work. We know it's you. Do you want to do this the easy way or the hard way?"

"What makes you think that website's mine?"

"We have our methods," Derek said. "Let's just say that nothing can ever be completely anonymous online. A month ago, we thought we'd found you. And placing a winner on your street to flush you out? Well, that confirmed it."

"Shall we try sodium thiopental on her?" Abby asked. "See if it'll make her talk?"

"No time for that now." Derek stood up, went to the blinds, and looked out. "It's getting dark soon." He looked down at the floor where Deanna and Ralph were tied up. "When it does, we're going to have to move you."

Ralph licked his lips. "Move us where?" he croaked. It was gratifying to know he could talk again.

Derek looked at his watch. "You shouldn't be able to talk yet. Looks like you might need another dart." Derek pulled the dart gun out of his pocket.

"You didn't answer the question," Ralph said. "Where are you moving Deanna and I?"

"Oh, not *you*," Derek said. "Just her. We don't need anything more from *you*, Ralph." He nodded toward Deanna. "But, you, Deanna, trust me, you don't *want* us to move you. If you want to avoid a lot of suffering, you can just give us the passwords to your website now, and I promise we'll make this as painless as possible for you. You can stay right here with your boyfriend. Die together."

"I don't know anything about a website," Deanna said.

Derek sighed. "I guess you're choosing the hard way." He turned to Abby. "You need to bring the car around out front."

Abby nodded and headed out the back.

Derek's phone rang. He began an incomprehensible acronym-laden conversation with HQ. When Derek wasn't looking, Ralph wormed his way closer to Deanna.

"Deanna," he whispered. "Can you reach in my right pocket?"

Deanna tried to move her hands, which were tied up behind her, over to Ralph's pockets.

"No. Can you scoot closer?"

Derek was still on the phone. He was looking out the blinds onto the street, apparently watching for Abby. Ralph shifted on his hip and tried to position his pocket as close as he could to where he assumed Deanna's hands would be. He felt her fingers reach in.

"Yeah. Got it."

"Can you get my car keys out?"

She fumbled around in his pocket and pulled them out.

"Got 'em."

It sounded like Derek was wrapping up. He was saying a lot of "yes, sirs" and "right away, sirs."

"As soon as he hangs up," Ralph said, "push the button on the back of the key. The one that's by itself. Just hold it down until—"

Derek hung up and turned around to face them.

"Now!" Ralph whispered.

The alarm started wailing on Ralph's car just outside. The horn honked, and the lights flashed.

"What the—?" Derek went to the door and opened it.

"Quick, push the button to open the doors," Ralph said. "It's on the other side of the key."

"Which one?" Deanna asked. "There's like four!"

"Just push everything!"

The minivan let out a series of beeps to warn that the side doors were sliding open.

Derek turned back to Ralph and Deanna.

"What are you up to?" he yelled. He noticed the keys in Deanna's hands. "Give me those!"

Derek bent over and reached down to grab the keys. His back was to the door, so he didn't see Burns galloping towards him, barking. Before Derek could react, Burns had rammed into Derek's rear end, knocking him down.

"Get him, Burnsie!" Ralph yelled out.

Burns was usually a friendly dog, but he was also intensely protective. He viciously pounced on Derek, knocking the dart gun out of his hands. While Burns bit and lunged and dodged and Derek tried to fight back, Ralph and Deanna struggled onto their knees. The car alarm kept honking.

Ralph crawled over to the kitchen counter. He wedged himself against the cabinets below the counter and pushed himself into a standing position. He reached behind himself with his bound-up hands and grabbed the scissors out of the knife block on the counter. "Come here! I'll cut your hands, and you cut mine!" he said to Deanna.

Derek was yelling and cursing as Burns continued to growl and attack.

Deanna crawled over and pushed herself up. They stood back to back. Ralph looked over his shoulder, trying to see what he was doing. It was harder than he thought. Ralph tried to tune out the noise from the honking and from Burns and Derek fighting so he could focus on getting those scissors onto Deanna's zipties. It took him three tries.

"Got it!" Ralph said. "Now do me!"

As Deanna grabbed the scissors, Ralph looked to see how Burns was doing. Burns had gained the initial advantage by knocking Derek into the ground. But Derek was bigger and stronger, and it didn't look like Burns would last much longer. At least Derek hadn't yet managed to pick up his dart gun or pull out a knife or a real gun or some other weapon.

Just as Deanna had cut the zip-ties around Ralph's wrists, he glanced through the kitchen window to see the grey sedan pull up. The driver's door flew open as Abby spilled out and ran towards the trailer.

Ralph pulled the ammo box out of his right pocket and the Glock out of his left. He managed to get two rounds into the magazine just as Abby came in the front door. He slammed the magazine back into the gun.

"What is going on, Derek? Half the neighborhood is looking out their windows right now! We've got to go—" Abby said, stopping just inside the front door.

"Burnsie, heel!" Ralph shouted, and the dog let loose of Derek's wrist and trotted over to stand at Ralph's side. "Hands up, now!"

Abby raised her hands. Deanna cut the zip ties off her ankles and then cut Ralph's. Derek was on his feet, moving toward Abby and the front door. He reached into his pocket.

"Hands up, now!" Ralph shouted.

Derek finally noticed that Ralph was armed. He put his hands up. Deanna retrieved her Taser from the ground, and then she pushed the button on the key to turn off the car alarm.

"Come in, Abby," Ralph said. "And close the door."

Deanna got more zip ties out of Derek's briefcase, and while Ralph kept his gun trained on them, he made Abby and Derek sit near the wall on Ralph's cheap folding chairs. Deanna zip-tied Derek's and Abby's wrists and ankles and emptied their pockets of cell phones and weapons, setting everything down on the kitchen counter. Deanna collected Derek's briefcase and Abby's handbag. Ralph talked soothingly to Burns, who had calmed down a little and was panting happily.

"Alright, start talking," Ralph said. "Tell us about the Annuity Squad."

"We're not saying anything," Abby said. "Your neighbors will come over soon to see what all this commotion was about. And when they do, how is it going to look when they see you holding a gun, with two people tied up in your house? You're the one who's in trouble right now. How about you let us go, and we forget that all of this ever happened?"

Ralph looked through the blinds out the window. "Now that the car alarm's off and Burns has calmed down, I don't think anything's going to happen. The neighbors have all stopped peeking out their windows. No one's out on the street. For them, it's just another day in the dumpiest trailer park in the city. I'm not worried about them at all. So, why don't you tell us who you really are?"

"We work for the National Publishers Company," Derek said calmly. "We're part of the Annuity Squad. All we do is help people sign up for their prizes."

"I bet your cell phones will prove otherwise," Deanna said, holding up Derek's and Abby's phones.

"There's nothing on there," Abby said. "Just standard text messages to Prize Posse HQ."

"And they're locked," Derek added.

"Oh really?" Deanna said. She stepped behind Abby, holding Abby's phone.

"What are you doing?" Abby asked.

Deanna said nothing and knelt. She put the phone up to Abby's index finger.

"Oh, just stealing your fingerprint," Deanna said. "And . . . the phone's unlocked. Gosh, that was easy," Deanna started tapping and swiping her fingers on the phone's screen. "Well, let's see what *is* on here."

Ralph kept his gun trained on Derek and Abby while Deanna checked the phone.

"Like I said," Abby replied. "Texts with Prize Posse HQ.

Oh, and my mom texted me a new cannoli recipe. It looks tasty. I can't wait to try it. Too bad you won't be able to. What with you getting arrested for kidnapping us and all."

Deanna looked up at Ralph. "She's right. Nothing in her texts so far . . . but let's see." Deanna tapped the screen a few more times. "Your Google Maps history matches up with the deaths I've tracked of the last five prize winners. Dates, times, and places are all perfectly in sync. I've got evidence now." She waved the phone at Derek and Abby.

"Start talking," Ralph said.

Derek laughed. "You mean a confession? Get serious. We're not confessing to anything."

"Hey, Deanna," Ralph said. "Could you please dump out Abby's handbag?"

"What's the matter? Run out of lipstick?" Abby taunted, but the look in her eyes showed worry.

"You mentioned sodium thiopental before," Ralph said. "I've read enough spy novels to know what that is. Truth serum. It's got to be in there somewhere."

Ralph watched the contents of Abby's purse spill across the counter as Deanna shook the bag.

"That looks promising." He pointed to a small metallic case. Deanna opened it. Inside was a glass vial of clear liquid and a syringe.

"Sodium thiopental," Ralph said, reading the side of the glass vial. "And the weapons you guys were carrying? That's enough to get the police *very* interested."

"Yeah," Derek sneered. "Just try it and see how well that works out for you. We've got *lots* of friends."

"Let's check his phone, too," Ralph said.

"It's locked, smart guy," Derek said.

"Well, good thing you're here to unlock it for us," Ralph said. "Or at least your fingerprints are."

A look of worry registered on Derek's face for just a split second. Then he laughed. "What makes you think I'd be dumb enough to make my phone unlockable with my fingerprint?"

"Can't hurt to check, can it?" Ralph said. "Deanna?"

Deanna nodded nervously. She eyed Derek and took a hesitant step forward.

"Don't worry," Ralph whispered to Deanna. "He's tied up. He can't manhandle you like he did before. But make sure to approach him from the side. If he does try something, I can keep a clear line of sight on his chest."

Deanna did as Ralph suggested and slowly walked toward Derek. She stopped at his side. She leaned back and looked behind him.

"He's clenching his hands," Deanna said. "I can't get to his fingers."

"Sounds like what you'd do if you had something to hide," Ralph said.

"You think I'm going to make this easy for you?" Derek asked.

Ralph looked at the counter and picked up Derek's tranquilizer dart gun with his left hand. "I suppose I could just shoot you with this."

"Alright, alright," Derek said with a mirthless laugh. "No need to take extreme measures." He turned to Deanna. "My hands are open. Give it a try, sugar."

Deanna again approached Derek from the side. She put the phone up to his index finger.

"Hey!" Deanna yanked the phone back and stood up. "He tried to grab the phone."

"Tighten his zip ties," Ralph said to Deanna. "Make it harder for him to grab."

Deanna grabbed the zip tie around Derek's wrists and yanked it tighter, "That's not too tight now, is it, sugar?" she asked, her voice dripping with sarcasm.

Ralph looked at Derek. "Last chance, man. If you don't open your hands and let her get your fingerprint, I'll shoot you with the tranquilizer gun. And I can vouch—it is *not* a fun experience."

"OK, fine," Derek said. "I've opened my hands."

Deanna bent over once more with the phone. "His right finger didn't work," Deanna said. "And neither did his left."

"See, told you," Derek said. "Not unlockable with fingerprints."

"Did you only try his index fingers?" Ralph said. "Try the other ones."

Once again, a look of worry flashed briefly across Derek's face. Deanna bent behind Derek and started trying his different fingers. Finally, the phone dinged.

"Got it!" Deanna said. "Just my luck—it was the last finger. Who uses their left pinky to unlock their phone, anyway?"

"Alright, you got me," Derek said. "Have fun reading *my* boring Prize Posse texts."

Deanna walked back over to Ralph. She browsed through his phone, "His maps app has incriminating locations, just like Abby's. But the texts and emails look like just mundane things about travel arrangements and stuff like that."

"No cannoli recipes?" Ralph asked.

"Very funny," Deanna said without looking up from the phone. "There's some emails with his buddies about going to the shooting range. And, hold on." She looked up at Derek. "Emails with your *writing* group? Derek, *you're* a writer? You don't strike me as the. . ." Deanna waved her hand as if searching for the right word, "as the artistic type."

Abby looked over at Derek. "Writing group? What's this?"

Derek's face flushed. "None of your business is what it is."

Deanna tapped on the phone's screen. "There's a whole folder in his email for it. Let's see. The first one is from his wife, saying she found an announcement at the local library about a writing group and signed him up."

"Big deal," Derek said, shrugging. "You know, she also texted me a shopping list last week. Be sure to check that out too. Spoiler alert—we were out of bananas!"

"Maybe," Ralph said. "But let's hear more about this writing group first." He motioned toward Derek with the gun. "So talk."

"You're pointing a gun at my face to hear about my writing group?" Derek asked.

When Ralph didn't respond, Derek continued, "Alright, whatever. There's not much to it. When my wife signed me up, I figured, why not give it a try? It turns out I have stories I want to tell, and my groupmates say I have a real talent for it. We write and share our pieces with each other. So what?"

"Well, let's have a look," Ralph said. "What do you think, Deanna? Let's see what he writes about."

Deanna scrolled for a second. "OK, hold on. Most of these look like they're from other members of his group—there's a vampire novel, a portal story, something about a fraternity, and . . . a memoir about Boy Scouts in the 1980s?" She looked up at Derek. "Is this *normal* for writing groups?" She shook her head and kept scrolling. "Ok, hold on, here's one from Derek." She paused and looked up at Ralph. "It's called 'Tales of a Private Assassin.'"

"Whoa," Ralph said.

Abby glared at Derek. "Are you kidding me?"

"It's all *fiction*," Derek said defensively. "None of this matters unless you all know a literary agent interested in a thriller with elements of dark comedy."

"Read a little—let's hear some of Derek's 'fiction,'" Ralph said to Deanna, making air quotes.

Deanna started reading:

Chapter One. Hollywood has *never* shown the reality of what it's like to be a government assassin. There's lots of waiting. Like staying out until the wee hours of the night tracking the target, so you can shoot him once he's finally alone on the street. But there's a lot more to it than even that. Shooting people on the street isn't how government assassins usually neutralize a target. They prefer things that won't be noticed. The big, showy jobs are usually only done to send a message. Like, "Don't steal important emails. And definitely don't leak them."

"Wait, did you kill—" Ralph interrupted.

"No, of course not," Derek said. "This is all fiction, remember?"

Deanna started reading again:

No, usually, we assassins do our jobs with a lot of finesse. Make it look like an accident. Like waiting in the hotel room of that investigative reporter and then making it look like he slit his wrists in the bathtub. And on a hard job, when it all comes together right, it's like art—poetry in motion.

There are other parts that Hollywood gets wrong about being a government assassin. There's lots of paperwork, and endless rules. Including about retirement. Have you ever wondered what happens to government assassins when they retire? The mandatory retirement age is 45. That's when good old Uncle Sam thinks that assassins don't have it in them anymore. For some of the female specialists, it's 30. Suddenly, they think you're too old to do the hard stuff.

Abby glared at Derek, then looked at Ralph and Deanna. "You guys are risking kidnapping and assault charges—and jail time—for amateur story hour?"

"Getting worried, Abby?" Ralph asked. "Deanna, want to hear more?"

"Definitely," Deanna said, looking up and shooting an icy stare at Derek. She looked down at the phone and started reading again:

> When the mandatory retirement age is that young, there's usually time for a second career. So, like most other bureaucrats, government assassins cash out and go to work in the private sector. The most ruthless assassin I ever knew became the successful owner of a car dealership. But most of the rest of us stay in the same line of work—assassins for hire. And most of us join outfits like the Annuity Squad.

"You used the name *Annuity Squad*?" Abby asked, disbelief in her voice. "Couldn't you have chosen a name different from, you know, *the place where you actually work*?"

"Fiction," Derek said. "It's all fiction, remember? Every writer can't help but include a few small, autobiographical elements. And my writing group has been loving this story."

Deanna continued reading:

> It's a big adjustment, switching to the private sector. Lots of changes. But one thing I don't miss about government work is the forms. First, you have to fill out a DNI-5641 Assassination Authorization Form. Then, once that's approved, comes the DNI-2298 Assassination Plan of Action Proposal. Once that's authorized comes the GS-9926 Equipment Requisition Forms, which are a nightmare. We all got excited when they an-

nounced they were introducing the GS-9926-EZ to 'simplify' the process, but that form actually ended up being two pages longer! And don't get me *started* on the DNI-116B Consolidated Expense Report and Request for Reimbursement After Assassination Mission. Heaven help you if you didn't get a receipt for something or if you claimed the wrong per diem rate. Yeah, that's one *great* thing about the private sector. Not only is the paperwork so much easier, but in the private sector, they let you get creative and improvise. A lot more freedom to do things your way. Smaller teams. 'Six-Sigma Agile' assassination, they call it in the corporate world.

But you know one of the hardest things about switching over to the private sector? Not as many gadgets. My favorite "tool" from government service was always the umbrella. It's one of those long umbrellas that looks like it could double as a walking stick. The tip of it conceals a syringe. All you need to do is, as you pass your target, touch the umbrella tip to his foot or his leg and push a button. A titanium micro-needle deploys and injects a special concoction that induces a heart attack about four hours later. The micro-needle is so tiny, it leaves no mark on the skin. The target can barely feel it puncturing the skin. Man, those gadgets were useful. The only problem with the umbrella gun was when you wanted to use it on a day with no rain.

Deanna paused and looked up from the phone. She shook her head, a look of disgust on her face. "Do you think this is funny? You're a monster. And a terrible writer. So far, if it wasn't for the incriminating evidence, I'd be bored stiff."

"Hey, it's just a first draft," Derek said. "I'm going to clean up the rough parts later."

"Just keep on reading," Ralph said.

"OK, OK," Deanna said, looking back down at the phone. She started reading again:

> But I'm happy in the corporate world. Annuity Squad does useful, productive work. We work for a sweepstakes company. It's all about minimizing costs. A long time ago, some hotshot MBA saw they were spending fifty million a year on sweepstakes prizes. He realized they could save a bundle by making sure they only awarded prizes to old people. They'd die sooner, ending their annuities. And that *did* keep costs down. The company was only paying out twenty million a year. But you know how these corporate types are. They've always got to make the next quarterly earnings statement better than the last. Someone realized that an assassination team would only cost seven million a year. That would save an extra thirteen million. And that savings translated into a *lot* of executive bonuses. So, that's where the Annuity Squad comes in. We're in charge of ensuring those annuity payments stay as low as possible. Dead people don't collect annuities. It's as simple as that.

"I can't believe you put all that in there," Abby said. "What an idiot!"

"You know what they say," Derek muttered. "Write what you know."

"Well, this is just great," Abby said. "I'm literally going to jail because my deluded partner thinks he's Hemingway or something. Only you could make a story about assassins sound this dumb."

Deanna kept reading:

> Originally, Annuity Squad was created as a subsidiary. But they spun it off as a separate company ages ago. The stock swap deal that year made a lot of money for the executives. And it's allowed us to diversify our assassination portfolio. We have lots of other clients now, too. We do work for lotteries, insurance companies, and other sweepstakes companies. You know, good, solid corporate clients. All the big companies rely on us for their assassination needs. We're the industry leader. Other outfits focus on political assassinations, foreign government work, and that kind of thing. But we're the big dog as far as corporate assassination goes.
>
> You might be wondering: how have these guys managed to get away with it for so long? Well, government assassins get excellent training. We're very surreptitious about it all. We know how to make a death look like natural causes. Or an accident. This kind of thing—fake 'accidents'— happens a lot more often than you'd think.

"Wow," Ralph said. "I can't believe you wrote this all down. This reads like a memoir. Not a novel." He looked at Deanna. "How much more is left?"

"It's long," Deanna said, scrolling. "It just goes on and on —" She put a hand to her mouth and started tearing up. "There's. . . there's a chapter about Gran. It even uses her real name," She looked up at Derek. "You *bastard.*"

Before Ralph could even react, Deanna grabbed her

Taser off the counter, bounded over to Derek, and gave him a long, painful jolt.

When she was through, and Derek was shuddering in his chair, she stood over him, sucking in deep breaths. "You're going to jail. And they're never going to let you out. If there's any justice in this world, you'll get the death penalty. How could you!?"

"Sounds like this book has all the evidence we need," Ralph said. "And full of facts the police can check out and verify."

"Derek, what were you *thinking*?" Abby said with disgust.

"No one at Annuity Squad or National Publishers Company was supposed to find out," Derek whimpered. "Like I said, this was a first draft. I was going to change all the names and identifying details in the final version."

"Why did you put real *names* in there?" Abby asked. "Hold on. Is my name in there?"

Derek just looked down and didn't answer.

"What *didn't* you put in there?" Abby continued. "Wait— did you write about *us*?" Abby's face flushed red. "Real smart, Derek. What's your wife going to think about this book, huh? I guess you won't be getting any conjugal visits in prison."

"Don't worry, we'll be fine," Derek said with false bravado. He looked over at Ralph and Deanna. "What do you think you're going to accomplish? Who's going to believe you? You know how crazy this all sounds, right? Abby and I are *not* the only Annuity Squad members, you know. And National Publishers Company is *not* going to be happy with you two. Neither will Annuity Squad. You guys are in real trouble."

"I think I have a solution for that, too," Ralph said.

"Oh yeah, how are you going to beat someone as ruthless and cold-hearted as a group of retired government assassins?" Derek asked.

"By finding someone even more ruthless and cold-hearted to help me," Ralph said.

* * *

One Year Later

Ralph and Deanna sat cuddled on the couch, watching TV. Ralph had one hand resting gently on Deanna's visibly protruding belly.

"Six months of being married," Deanna sighed. "Who'd have thought we'd end up here?"

Ralph looked around at their new 10,000-square-foot luxury home. "The movers did a good job getting us set up in here. You'd never think that we just moved in two weeks ago."

"Well, it helps when you can pay for the best. But are you sure your kids like their new rooms?"

"Are you kidding? They *love* them, almost as much as the huge playset out back."

Just then, Burnsie came in through his doggie door and sat down on the couch beside Ralph. He gave Burnsie a scratch behind the ear for being a good boy.

A commercial came on TV. A serious-looking man in a nice business suit stood in front of a dark mahogany bookcase full of matching leather-bound books with gilded lettering. He spoke with a stern, no-nonsense tone.

"Have you lost a loved one after a payout from a sweepstakes, lottery, or insurance company? You may be entitled to substantial financial compensation. Call us at 1-800 . . ."

A number flashed on-screen.

Ralph and Deanna looked at each other and smiled.

"Thank God for lawyers," Ralph said.

He turned off the TV. They were going to bed early that night.

To sign up for this author's email newsletter and receive a free short story as a thank you, go to
JamesKennethRogers.com/Newsletter

The Theatrica Mechanica

by Eric Nilles

Imagine, if you are able, a machine so splendid it incorporates seventy musical automatons rivaling the King's royal orchestra. Combine that with miniature moving castles, countless marching foot soldiers, automatous knights in full armor, beasts of all varieties, fleets of small floating ships rowed autonomously, a theater, a dash of comedy here and a few small explosions there; Thus is the nature of the Theatrica Mechanica, an enormous contraption renowned far and wide, throughout all of upper Geratias. It is said that whispers of the device's existence have even reached as far as the southern fingerlands.

At the Theatrica Mechanica's core is a clock, a masterful timepiece, of course, but it's also so much more, tracking the phases of the moons, the positions of the six planets, and the constellations via large marbles that move along raceways. Through the use of what its maker calls "instruments of detection," it predicts the ideal time to sow and to reap the harvest with amazing accuracy. It has been informing and entertaining the masses in the King's courtyard for decades.

All the wonders of the Theatrica Mechanica are the product of one man's work – Lambert the Tinkerer. Lambert's appointed purpose at birth was to be educated in the creation of masterpieces of rhythmic cam ticking, pendulum swinging, and cog clackery. King Bartkull, of the Seventh Realm, sent Lambert at the age of seven to the far east to master, if one could, the art of automatous tinkering, sparing no expense in cultivating him into a servant who could create the contraptions the King desired.

Throughout his life of service to the king, Lambert created many clocks, musical fountains, calliopes and automated devices of various kinds, powered by woundspring, wind, water, weights and occasionally fire, but the work of creating his magnum opus consumed him for 21 years, tinkering and toiling, scavenging bits and pieces from the King's sculptors, collecting exploding potions from the King's sorcerer, commissioning the hammering out of myriad ironworks to exacting specifications by the King's royal blacksmiths. Taking no wife and fathering no children, he dedicated much of his life to the building of the mighty Theatrica Mechanica.

When it was finally finished, a team of fourteen oxen was required to drag it on a platform of rolling logs to the palace, to the King's great hall, where it was ceremoniously presented before both king and country.

The Theatrica Mechanica resides in the place of highest honor, where most other kings would have chosen to place their thrones. But so impressed was King Bartkull by Lambert's device that he had his royal carpenters shift his throne off to the side, yielding to Lambert's great machine.

Cogs are always turning within the Theatrica Mechanica, as are its massive row of pendulums swinging at various speeds, and its marbles which roll down raceways, clicking into their proper places as the contraption counts off the minutes of the days. Each hour is marked differently: at the first hour past midnight the timing door opens and a mouse sneaks out to find a bit of bread; the second hour an enormous mechanical cricket, the size of a medibeast, gently rubs its legs together in a nighttime melody.

It's not until the eighth hour that a more significant noise is made by the machine as a rooster emerges from the timing door announcing the hour of morning. The ninth hour is marked by the growl of the burrowbear, and the tenth by the brash cuckoo's call, and so on.

But on the seventh hour past noon of every seventh day, the Theatrica Mechanica enters into "Eruption Mode." Many subjects of the kingdom, sometimes along with travelers from surrounding kingdoms, gather at this hour to witness the contraption's true spectacle, which is always unique and never fails to surprise and amaze.

Most eruptions begin with the whirring of gears and puffs of steam as the Theatrica unfolds itself in some way, revealing perhaps a miniature battlefield, or a colorful village, or even an ancient forest full of elusive creatures. Some weeks automatous figurines with weapons fight in mock battles. During some eruptions, the dwellings and castles slide away and the battlefield is flooded. Battleships row out, sailors flash their swords at one another and miniature cannons fire their reports.

Every eruption is begun and concluded with an orchestral arrangement, written by the King's own master musician and delivered to Lambert well ahead of time, whereby Lambert would examine the notes on the page and then measure out the sands and modify the many cam wheels that drove his automatons to play their instruments.

King Bartkull always had his workers partition off the Theatrica as Lambert prepared his device. So in love with his work was Lambert that he would often start whistling the tunes he was programming his half-scale orchestra to perform. Often the King, with a jolly laugh and a wink, would catch his subjects eavesdropping on Lambert's whistling. Some were in the habit of hurrying to their homes and plucking away at their lutes and lyres, trying to reproduce Lambert's notes from memory so they could parade around the streets, gossiping and playing the tunes in advance, as if they had some form of clairvoyance into the matter. Yet the King didn't mind this behavior at all. He simply enjoyed having people come to his great hall so he could bend their ears bragging about his Theatrica Mechanica.

Almost always, foreign visitors, overcome with amazement, would beg to look further into the machine, yearning for just a glimpse of what precisely makes Lambert the Tinkerer's curious contraption work.

"The inner workings and wonders of this machine are proprietary, my dear guests," King Bartkull would always explain, nodding his guards to urge away those who became too curious.

The Theatrica Mechanica's greatest admirer might have been the King's beautiful daughter, Princess Vesponika. Ropes partitioned the Theatrica Mechanica from its audience, but from childhood the princess had been allowed to sit on the floor in front of the ropes to admire the mechanical wonder up close. She had an acute fascination with the machine, often shirking her normal princessly duties of appearing here and there in the kingdom by chariot in the company of her father.

"Am I just an accessory to you?" She would always retort in response to her father questioning her about her frequent absences, to which he would reply, "Well, since your mother the Queen has passed... yes. The kingdom expects it."

One particular day, when the temperature had warmed pleasantly and the sun was only interrupted by an occasional billowy cloud, the King's chariot appeared over the grassy knoll just outside the castle. Vesponika, who had been reclining under a Zizzlefruit tree enjoying one of its delicious red fruits, saw her father's chariot approach. She jumped to her feet, dropping the fruit, having in mind to abscond quickly.

But the King saw his daughter and ordered his driver to stop. He leapt out of the chariot, calling her over with folded arms and a furrowed brow. Once Vesponika was in the chariot, he ordered his driver to continue.

"It's a short trip to the castle, Father," Vesponika said

with a pout. "I think I could have managed."

King Bartkull said, "You knew you were to accompany me in my travels today, yet you were nowhere to be found when I left this morning."

"I'm sorry, but Lambert needed my help with the Theatrica Mechanica."

"Oh he did, did he." The King said, stroking the tip of his salt-and-pepper beard. "Vesponika, you are to become queen someday." he took her hand and examined it. "You must practice the part. And look at your lovely hand, soiled with grease."

"It's eruption night, Father. Lambert was fashioning the cogs," she said, excitement shining in her striking hazel eyes.

King Bartkull couldn't help but smile at her lovingly as he pulled her close, kissing the top of her light brown hair. "Yes, of course you were. See to it that your maidens scrub thoroughly under your nails and dress you in your blue dress for tonight's eruption. There can be left not one scrap of evidence that I allow you to tinker as you do."

As the King sat on the throne that night, with Princess Vesponika in her beautiful blue dress, off her throne and sitting close to the Theatrica Mechanica as usual, Chancellor Patherin, the King's most trusted advisor, came to him with a troubled look. "May I suggest we speak in the hall, my Lord?"

The King followed Patherin into the passageway. "What is it?"

Patherin spoke softly. "Forgive me for interrupting the prelude, my Lord, but the matter at hand is of utmost importance. Our scouts have returned from the south. Haver's realm has been swallowed up by the Southern King, Pompeus the Younger."

"Swallowed up? That's not possible."

"But I'm afraid it is, my Lord. I have personally interviewed witnesses, a few poor refugees from Haver's kingdom who consider themselves lucky to have escaped with their lives. King Haver, your ally, has been beheaded. His kingdom is no more."

"Beheaded!" Bartkull said, screwing up his face, rubbing his hands together fretfully. "That's just so... hard to believe. Haver prided himself on his military. He, he had twice the manpower of our kingdom."

"Haver's mighty army fell. His treasure rooms have been plundered. Only selected young women and children, it seems, escaped death, being carried off to the south. All other subjects of Haver's kingdom were put to the sword.

"This explains why his dignitaries never showed for the eruption."

"Very much so, my Lord."

King Bartkull removed his gold crown and began fidgeting with the rubies. "Pompeus is a vile king, executing his enemies in defecation pits and that sort of thing. In the south, among those numberless realms, his conquests have become legion. But I never suspected his ambitions would meander as far north as Haver's kingdom. My goodness, with Haver's demise, it will be but a matter of time before Pompeus moves on us. We must prepare for the worst, I'm afraid. Send a messenger to summon Quagley. With him I must consult."

The King returned to his hall, shifting endlessly, as if his throne had suddenly become uncomfortable. He seemed disconnected from the show at hand, his thoughts consumed by the terrible fate of his friend and ally.

Later that night, as the eruption concluded, the Theatrica Mechanica's small stage went dark and its curtain closed. The stage retracted back into the machine. The audience filed out of the hall, the candles were extinguished, and the King sat on his throne, alone in the darkness.

* * *

Permeating Quagley's cave was the gentle nibbling sound

of fluvals fattening themselves on the fodder the wizard had dumped into their enclosure. It was a pleasant change from the incessant hunger squeaks the furry little creatures had been bothering him with minutes earlier.

From a hole in the stone wall, a raven named Babbs shuffled out sideways onto a perch hung from the cave's ceiling, nabbing with his beak a piece of fish the wizard had dropped into his bowl. Quagley gave the bird a gentle pat on the head.

Feeding all the creatures allowed Quagley, for the first time in hours, to finally sit at his desk in peace and thoroughly examine the curious book he had stumbled upon earlier in the day, acquiring it in a trade with a wagon of nomads for but a tiny flask of sleeping potion. Quagley grinned, ruminating on his good fortune in the bargain.

His desk had been fashioned from the twin stumps of a pair of lovewood trees, the branches of which had grown together at the lap, locked forever in their entangled embrace the day they were felled as one. Quagley leaned his twisted wooden staff against the desk, where it fit into a groove, looking as if it had been one of the tree's many branches.

"Flamespread," he said. A candle that had been burning on the desk began to sizzle. Small cinders popped out of the flame, floating over to two separate collections of candles of varying heights and widths, one to his right and the other to his left. The candles to his right sat upon a natural stone formation within the cave. The ones to his left were atop a shelf where he kept many of his non-flammable potions and various minerals of importance. The small, floating cinders, perhaps forty in all, gently settled onto the wicks of all these candles. Most candles started flames, although a few failed to ignite. Nevertheless, the cave was suddenly cast in a warm glow.

Quagley leaned forward, inspecting the mess of raggedy-looking pages of parchment resting upon his desk. His first task would be to ascertain the order of the pages. The book was so ancient the binding had completely disintegrated, leaving it just a collection of scribed pages held together with a length of twine tied in a bow. If he could succeed at putting the pages in their proper order, he could then figure out if any pages were missing.

The book's cover had been lost, but he was almost sure it was a sort of instruction manual on conjuring swarms of insects, a subject matter that might be well worth the toil. If fully translated from its ancient dialect, it would become, perhaps, more valuable than gold. Like all good wizards, Quagley knew the most obscure abilities could sometimes be put to use in unexpected ways, presenting solutions to the most curious predicaments.

Pulling the twine, Quagley untied the bow, releasing the papers. Blowing a lock of long, grey hair off his face, he picked up one particular page, scrutinizing its faded ink through a large magnifying glass. "Hmpf," he said, flipping it over, poring over the back.

Babbs "Cawed," rocking back and forth on his perch.

A sudden *boing* drew both Quagley and Babb's eyes toward the mouth of the cave. Due to a curve in the cavern, the entrance was out of sight, but Quagley knew the sound well, recognizing it as someone, or something, encountering with surprise his security bubble, which was virtually invisible in the dusk.

"Who goes there?" he called out.

"Jessup, sir. Herald of the King, with a message for Quagley, the King's sorcerer."

"That's me," Quagley sighed. Pulling his staff from its groove in the desk, he pointed it slightly at the entrance of the cave. "Release!" Then he returned to his examination of the page.

Jessup cautiously walked into the cave, feeling in front of him for further bubbles with one hand while holding his nose with the other. Stepping fully into the candlelight, he said, "The King has sent..."

"Not yet," said Quagley with a palm up. He set down his magnifying glass and eagerly dipped his quill in an inkwell, fervently scratching notes on a paper.

From deep within the bowels of the cave came a great roar.

Jessup stiffened, afraid to move. "Wh... what was that?"

The fluval creatures stopped their feeding, quickly absconding into burrows within the bedding of their enclosure. Babbs disappeared into his hole.

Quagley jammed his quill back in its holder with a touch of aggression, scowling at the King's scribe. "Something that has caught a whiff of what it presumes to be its next meal."

Jessup put a quivering hand to his chest. "Do you mean me?"

"I do," said Quagley, with what might have been a faint smile.

"Please, sir, I fear for my life. Tell me, what dreadful beast do you keep that would make a meal of me?"

"Trust me, the less you know of a wizard's business, the better. But rest assured... forgive me, what did you say your name was?"

"Jessup, sir."

Quagley leaned his staff back against his desk, swung his legs out from under it, and stood, cinching the belt of his tattered indigo robe. "Ah, yes, Jessup, of course. Rest assured, while I'm here, you are *not* in danger." Quagley glanced toward the bowels of his cave and the source of a more subtle growl, this time coming from the beast's stomach. "Well, probably not."

Jessup crouched, slowly easing back toward the cave's entrance.

Quagley frowned, pushing his fists into his hips. "A bit jittery to qualify as a King's herald, aren't we?"

"Sorry, sir. It was only this morning I received my appointment."

"Well then, come out with it, Jessup. What message do you bring from our King?"

Jessup straightened himself. "Oh, yes, um... Our southern allies have all been conquered. Pompeus and his army march north. The King suspects he will move on our kingdom soon. He urgently requests your counsel."

Quagley's eyes went wide. "Ancient master of Wizardry!" he said, a phrase he often uttered in times of stress. "Next time you bring news of this magnitude, lead with it!"

"Y... yes, sir."

"This matter is urgent," Quagley said, swiftly fetching his staff and his conical hat, waving a hand along the way, extinguishing all the candles into trails of smoke and leaving the cave in just the dim, reddish glow from a lantern hung from the ceiling. "Quickly, to our horses. We must ride through the night."

* * *

Quagley burst into the great hall, urgently hurrying to the King's throne, bowing his head. "My Lord, I came immediately."

The King asked a few subjects to leave and motioned to Quagley to skip the pleasantries. "I'll get right to it. Not a year has passed since Pompeus the Younger ran his father through with the sword, assuming control of the southern realms. Now, it appears, he has become overly ambitious. As you may know, last year I sent 300 men to fight alongside our ally, King Rostraus of the First Realm. None of those men returned, and no news of their fate has ever found us. I've always suspected Pompeus was somehow behind their disappearance.

"Two nights ago, on the night of eruption, I learned that Pompeus had swallowed up Haver's kingdom – our strongest ally. There was no provocation. Haver was given no warning, no opportunity for negotiation. They say Pompeus personally took pleasure in the torture and execution of the innocent of Haver's king-

126

dom, impaling wives before their husbands, and children before their mothers. His evil knows no boundaries."

Quagley leaned on his staff, lowering his eyes. "Very unfortunate, my Lord."

"Indeed. And how long until he moves on us? I have sent scouts to assess his numbers, and I have warned our knights to keep a watchful eye. Our fighting men, yes even our young boys, are being trained as we speak. But, still, I am hopeful that you could conjure something that might save us from this turmoil."

"Honorable King Bartkull, I will enchant the archer's arrows and strengthen any new blades your blacksmiths have forged, of course, but I doubt anything I do will be enough. Pompeus the Younger is in league with nine urklings!"

"Urklings!"

"Yes. Nine of them. Quite the unholy number."

"From where?"

"Some from here, my Lord, who have now learned to draw their magic from the dark watchers. We should have destroyed them, but when they knelt before you, kissing your scepter of mercy, accepting exile from our forests, where did you expect them to go? North, to the frigid lands? No. Trickled down to Pompeus they did."

The King gazed forlornly through an opening in the castle wall, up into a sky overcast with dark clouds that churned tumultuously in the throes of an approaching storm. "By my mercy, I have strengthened my enemy."

"Unfortunately, yes."

He turned back to Quagley. "Can we defeat them?"

"Not by magic, I'm afraid. I could have quickly dispatched of them individually, but in darkness they have joined forces, mastering the art of wielding as one. I have sensed their union through the veins of Geratias." Quagley sighed. "I'm afraid their power has grown far beyond mine."

Lambert the Tinkerer, who had been tuning and oiling the Theatrica Mechanica as he often did, couldn't help but overhear the conversation occurring between his King and the Wizard Quagley. He approached slowly with his head bowed low until he caught the attention of both. They stopped talking, looking at him expectantly.

"Forgive me, my King, but I couldn't help but overhear a few details of the grave situation we find ourselves in."

"Speak freely, Lambert," said the King.

"I offer a possible solution to our predicament, although I'll admit it to be a bit unorthodox."

After hearing Lambert's plan, King Bartkull immediately locked the doors of the great hall, keeping the room clear for Lambert the Tinkerer and the Wizard Quagley to begin work on the Theatrica Mechanica. Even Vesponika was forbidden to enter the chamber, much to her chagrin.

The King clasped and rubbed his hands, moving here and there to gain good vantage points as he watched his wizard and his tinkerer climb into, over, and even under the Theatrica Mechanica. They worked through a storm that lasted all day and into the night. The King himself held a lantern, positioning and re-positioning it as Quagley and Lambert toiled well beyond the midnight hours.

The King, the tinkerer and the wizard scarcely slept as their hours and days were spent preparing and modifying the Theatrica Mechanica. Servants merely set food, changes of clothing, and supplies at the great hall's entrance, for the three had taken up residence there tenaciously, refusing to retire for even a few hours to proper bed chambers. After three days, Quagley departed on the King's best horse for his cave, returning the next day with a few items that only he could procure.

On the seventh day of all this tinkering, a bright morning sunlight shone through the high openings in the wall of the great hall, casting angled columns of light through a mist of steam and oil that filled the room from testing certain functions of the Theatrica Mechanica.

Patherin, the King's advisor, knocked on the door with his secret knock.

A tired and weary King unlocked the door for him. "Come, Patherin, come. What news have you?"

Upon entering, Patherin wrinkled his nose – likely a response to a slightly acrid smell of machinery, and perhaps wizardry, that hung in the air, of which the others had simply grown accustomed. He quickly corrected himself and bowed before his King. "My Lord, we have just received a messenger from the garrison Southport. Pompeus the Younger has attacked. The garrison is lost. Only the messenger survived. Everyone else was put to the sword."

Lambert the Tinkerer rested his grimy hands on the work of his lifetime, craning his neck, awaiting the King's response to Patherin's revelation. Quagley the Wizard wiped his hands of grease, taking up his staff and clicking it on the floor.

The King swallowed hard, shifting his gaze to his wizard and his tinkerer at the Theatrica Mechanica. "Well, is it ready?"

"It is," said Lambert with what might have been feigned confidence.

The King turned sullenly, staring at the castle's stone floor, to a small spot where a patch of moss flourished between the cobbles. "We have but a few hours. Open the doors. Summon the masons. We must act quickly."

The King turned to Quagley. "Signal the heralds. Everyone not selected to remain must leave for the mountains of evermore. All their preparations have been for this moment. Tell them time is short. They should carry only what they need, and fire to keep warm."

Quagley took his staff to the end of the great hall, to the

round wall, the stones of which supported the castle's highest spire. Touching his staff to the stones, he called out an incantation. A few purple sparks left his staff, jumping into the mortar between stones, running like little rivers up the wall and through the ceiling, making their way up through the spire to the copper roof.

The purple sparks sizzled along the green copper spire, igniting a volley of reports and explosions that immediately garnered the attention of the village below. The explosions were well known to the King's subjects, but were typically more colorful, announcing the birth of a child or the wedding of a young couple. But on this day, Quagley's sparks cast the streets in a red hue, filling everyone with dread as they knew it announced the coming of the evil King Pompeus, and that they were to flee their homes. The Heralds, seven young riders who had been anticipating the signal, mounted their horses forthright and quite nimbly kicked their heels, driving their horses like lightning, thundering over the drawbridge and into the countryside, proclaiming, "Pompeus' army is near! Flee to the place only our people know! Take only what you can carry!"

* * *

The King left his chambers, walking the hallway proudly, with a lone servant to carry his sword and helmet. He re-entered the great hall he'd only left a few hours before. To his left was his throne platform, empty, abandoned of any advisors. To his right, the chairs of his musicians and the benches of his court were all empty. Before him, a handful of loyal subjects who remained behind bowed. At some distance beyond them was a new wall covering the Theatrica Mechanica.

The King motioned for his stone masons to end their bows. They were tired and weary, their clothing smeared with mortar and drenched with sweat. "Go, flee, meet up with your families."

"As you wish, my King," they all said, bowing their heads

one last time before clumsily absconding.

With his staff, Quagley lit a fire in the fireplace. "Fire will aid in curing the mortar and also draw out some of the fumes."

"Good idea, Quagley." Bartkull said, accepting his sword and his helmet from his servant, sheathing the sword, and carrying the helmet under his arm. He walked to his remaining subjects, greeting each of them. Then he watched as his knights knelt in a circle in the middle of the room. Each of these remaining knights had been hand-selected, more for their willingness to sacrifice than their ability to fight. They all drew their swords, touching the tips to a circular pattern inlaid into the cobbles of the floor and resting their palms nervously on the pommels. This act was the kingdom's tradition before war.

The King, dressed in silver chainmail as were his knights, put on his helmet and knelt with them, drawing his sword and touching it to the circle as they had. Quagley reclined in an empty chair near the fire, humming some old, somber tune. And there they waited. As the sun traversed the sky, a red ruby in the pommel of the King's ornate sword gathered light from an opening in the wall, winking and twinkling far too playfully for the mood in the room.

The King lifted his visor and stared somberly at Fordley. The gray, feeble knight had begun trembling, causing his chainmail to jingle.

"Fordley," the King's voice croaked.

Fordley lifted his head, nervously stroking his long grey beard which extended out under his helmet, and stared at his counterparts in turn, seemingly annoyed to find himself the center of attention. He shifted his gaze to his King. "Yes, my Lord."

"Your armor quivers. Are you alright?"

"My apologies, my Lord, but this helmet is heavy, and I grow weary waiting to die."

The King removed his helmet. The silver knights followed his lead, setting their helmets on the floor. Then the King said, "My dear Fordley, you have served this kingdom your entire life, even under my father. Your end draws near, as it does for us all. But if you do not wish to drink this cup, you are free to take your horse and flee. But if you stay, your sacrifice will not go unrewarded, for I tell you, in the kingdom to come I will be your servant," he looked at the others, "Yes, I will serve you all in the life to come, for my time to be served concludes this day. But we will all be the masters of whatever remains of this kingdom, because it is only through our sacrifice that the kingdom will live on.

Fordley leaned on his sword, his eyes sifting the thoughts of a brutal demise sure to be filled with pain and agony. Then he stood, gazing into the others with a look of bewilderment on his face. He glanced over at the wizard, who had stopped humming, listening intently for Fordley's response.

After much hesitation in Fordley's response, Quagley shot him a look of surprise. "The plan is sound, Fordley. Stay the course."

"I'm sorry Quagley, and my Lord," he said, trembling. "But I am too old. Yes, too old to die!" He stumbled to his feet, limped to the doors of the great hall, flung them open and absconded without so much as a look back.

The King stood, slamming the door shut in disgust. "Let him go. Too old to die, indeed. Anyway, now there are but seven of us with swords."

"And I with my staff," added Quagley.

"Yes, of course," said the King.

"And I, with my Theatrica Mechanica," called out the faint voice of Lambert the Tinkerer, from within the newly constructed stone wall that completely enclosed both him and his machine.

The King fetched his crown from its place beside the throne, affixing it to his head and walking over to a small hole left

132

in the wall so Lambert could breathe. A few knights wandered to his side. The King looked upon the wall his masons had hastily completed, feeling a seam of mortar, still moist and uncured. "Don't lean on it. The mortar is still wet."

Then he spoke into the hole in the wall. "Don't be nervous, Lambert, for if Pompeus has any brains in his skull you will be the only one of us to survive. The work of your lifetime, endless years of tinkering, have brought such joy to my life, and to Vesponika, and everyone in this fine kingdom. Now, it will be our salvation! Yes, because of your great machine, a remnant of us will go on."

"Keep the potion near," Quagley reminded Lambert. "Drink it only at the appointed time, for it will only protect for one-quarter hour."

Just then, Princess Vesponika barged in, crying, "Father!"

The King whipped his neck at the voice of his daughter, wheeling around, screaming, "Why are you here?"

"I have returned for you. Why have you not left with us, Father?"

The King embraced his daughter. "This is the only way to save the kingdom. But you're not supposed to be here!"

"Father, I want you to come with me right now."

The King hugged his daughter, breathing in the lovely aroma of his child's hair, perhaps for the last time. Then he held her back and looked into her eyes, his eyes flowing like two rivers. "If I move to preserve my life, Pompeus will pursue our people, Vesponika. Don't you see? I have chosen to lay down my life for my people. And you now stand in my way!"

Vesponika pounded her fist on his metal-clad chest, ringing the chainmail like a hundred bells. "Come with me, Father. Come with me this moment."

Distraught with emotion, the King turned to one of the knights and said, "Quick, a few old mares are left in the stable.

Take Vesponika to Evermore."

Inside the wall, the Theatrica Mechanica's cogs were turning, announcing the ninth hour with the hiss of the granderserpent.

It was at that very moment that Chancellor Patherin, the King's advisor, barged into the hall. "Too late! Too late! Pompeus and his men are in the bailey. I spied them through an archer's slot."

King Bartkull ran to the window. Stealing a quick glance down, he saw Pompeus' soldiers creeping throughout the bailey with shields and swords, testing doors and passages to see which were latched, ever expectant of resistance that would never come. An old horse in the stable neighed and bucked at its binding as a soldier waved his sword nearby.

Bartkull rushed to the other side of the hall, looking out over the grasslands, and found an army more massive than any he'd ever imagined treading heavily on the lands, with countless beasts of burden lugging massive catapults and siege towers. Pompeus' army had entered his kingdom faster than he'd ever realized any army could.

Bartkull sank under the window pane, wailing, "Why, Vesponika? Why did you come back?"

She went to him, flinging her arms around him, crying now that she understood it would be the end for both of them.

"Might I offer a suggestion?" said Quagley.

"What is it, Quagley? What could possibly help us in this predicament?"

"If I can get close enough, and if I survive long enough, I might be able to charm Pompeus with my enamoring incantation." He rolled his eyes, looking as if an explanation was owed, and as if the King would care under the current duress. "It's a specialty of mine. I've used it for years." He cleared his throat, looking a bit embarrassed. "Anyway, If Pompeus is smitten with her, he may yet spare her."

"Oh, that would be horrible. Worse than death. My daughter, bound to the will of that vile Pompeus. Worse than death, I tell you."

"Remember, my Lord, if everything goes according to plan, it will only be for a few days."

The King looked at his beautiful daughter Vesponika, her flowing hair and those big hazel eyes that reminded him so much of her mother. He cringed at the thought of Pompeus' murderous hands dragging her from this kingdom, from everything she knew, using her as a common harem servant. "Over my dead body," he said out of habit, a moment before realizing this time it would likely be the exact circumstances of her departure.

He sighed, closing his eyes. "Do what you must," he muttered.

Quagley stepped forward to Vesponika. "Forgive me, my princess," he said, plucking a few hairs from her head. He held them in the cup of his hand, touched the head of his staff to them, and said, "Markessence."

The hairs morphed into a sparkling glow. A moment later the glow was absorbed by Quagley's staff.

"That will have to do," Quagley said as he rushed to the door. Through the peephole he heard the hoofs of powerful horses clip-clopping through the castle's passageways. He watched Pompeus's infamous Black Knights turn the corner, cautiously creeping toward the hall, pointing their weapons offensively into every nook and corridor, prepared for a volley of swords or arrows that never came. One knight's halberd caught on one of the many tapestries that hung along the castle's passageways, tearing it and sending it crumpled to the stone floor to then be trampled under muddy hoofs.

"Knights approach," Quagley announced.

"Unlock the door," The King ordered.

Quagley removed the door timber and retreated as an iron-tipped spear was thrust through the peephole, narrowly missing him. Just then a torturous neigh rang out, as if from a horse rearing up on its hind legs The doors sprang open with a thunderous crackle. A Black Knight surged into the great hall.

Sparks like lightning burst from Quagley's staff, striking the Knight in his armored breastplate, knocking him from his horse.

The next Black Knight galloped in, but one of Bartkull's silver knights ambushed him with an upward thrust of his sword, only himself to be struck down by the long reach of a halberd from a third intruder.

After that, Black Knights poured into the great hall, quickly outnumbering them.

Bartkull's five remaining Silver Knights retreated to the circle in the floor, doing their best to surround Quagley, Platherin and Vesponika.

"Laso inpenatre," said Quagley. Something like a translucent film rose from the circle inlaid on the floor, closing over their heads, encapsulating them within. Light flickering from the fireplace, and from the torches of the foot soldiers who now entered the room, reflected off Quagley's translucent film, as light from a lantern might reflect in a bubble floating in a mug of barley grog – only Quagley's bubble was massive.

One silver knight removed a small dagger from a sheath on his calf, handing it to Patherin. Patherin looked at his hand as if he'd been handed a toad. Nevertheless, he decided to turn aggressively toward the invaders, holding the dagger all wrong, of course.

The Black Knights surrounded the bubble, parading around it slowly, inspecting it only through the slats in their visorless helmets. It was well known that Pompeus's kingdom considered it a great dishonor for its Black Knights to show their faces or even to speak. Legends tell of the knights having their armor riveted in place onto their bodies, with no way to remove it, even during sleep.

The Black Knights decided to test Quagley's bubble, wielding their swords and halberds onto it, but the weapons just clanged off as if it was the thickest of armor. An archer with a crossbow aimed and fired an iron-tipped arrow at the bubble, but a ricochet sent it striking the flank of one of the Black Knight's horses, just under its armor. The horse did not kick or reel up as one would expect from a horse – but they were no ordinary horses.

This particular Black Knight, who wielded a mace rather than a sword, extracted immediate revenge for the injury of his horse, striking down the archer who shot the arrow.

The Black Knights held up their horses, resting their weapons on their oily saddles. The foot soldiers lowered their crossbows and rested their halberd staffs on the floor. The hall quieted as all of them, apparently emotionless by the ease at which Quagley's bubble thwarted their efforts, seemed content to wait endlessly. All that could be heard was the breathing of the horses and the crackle of the fireplace.

Suddenly the horses parted. The great hall's entrance was once again visible to King Bartkull. "Does your King Pompeus now come to face me?" Bartkull bellowed.

Instead, urklings drifted into the room. If it wasn't for the occasional kick of feet within the edges of their tattered gray robes, one might think the urklings floated as they moved about, for such was how they moved. They formed up around Quagley's bubble.

Princess Vesponika peeked out from behind her father, gasping at the sight of the urklings. Bartkull himself winced at the sight of their burned and disfigured faces, for these creatures now bore little resemblance to anything he had once expelled from his kingdom.

"I wield through my staff for my own protection," Quagley explained to his King and the others in his bubble. "But these creatures have no sense of self-preservation, for as you will see, in their lust for power they wield directly."

The urklings, nine in all, raised their hands – or rather what was left of them, for their extremities had been burned and disfigured, with some missing finger parts. Red lights of power flowed from the hands of the urklings, not quickly like lightning, but flowing slowly, as water through a trickling brook, ending and spreading upon the surface of Quagley's bubble. The bubble took on a reddish hue, but otherwise seemed unaffected.

"You'll learn nothing from that," said Quagley, winking smugly at the urklings.

The Black Knights and foot soldiers made way as the urklings began to parade around the bubble, chanting out incantations in unison, each incantation manifesting itself as a slight change of hue in the fingers of power that seemed to be testing and searching the bubble for weaknesses. It concluded with a sudden burst that seemed to increase in intensity, as if the urklings were expressing frustration, or perhaps rage. Quagley's staff swayed a bit, but his bubble held.

Smoke wafted in trails from the disfigured hands of the Urklings, carrying with them the rank of burning flesh, leaving no doubt as to why their hands had become disfigured in the first place.

"They reek of burning flesh," The princess scowled.

"Shush, child," said Quagley, removing a hand from his staff, whisking Vesponika behind him until she was barely visible between him and the others.

"Remember," Bartkull reminded them all, speaking quietly so only those within the bubble would hear, "The Theatrica Mechanica is what's important now. Our deaths must be convincing if this plan is to work and if our people are to survive."

"Show us your king," yelled Bartkull defiantly to the urklings, knights, and soldiers that surrounded them, "And I will have my sorcerer drop his shield."

From somewhere outside, a deep, flat-noted horn sounded. The Black Knights dismounted their horses and formed a sort of gauntlet at the hall's entrance. The knights, urklings, and soldiers knelt and bowed their heads.

A man of average stature walked in, bearing black armor similar to the knights, but instead of a helmet, a black crown sat atop his head. He held no weapon or shield. His youthful brown beard was patchy and unkempt. He approached Quagley's bubble with his chest puffed out and a gleam in his eye.

"What's this game you play, Bartkull? No archers? No one to man your catapults? Have your swordsman abandoned you, leaving you with just these few feeble knights and an old wizard to defend your kingdom?"

"Pompeus the Younger, I presume," said King Bartkull.

He showed a crooked grin. "You presume correctly."

"When I last saw you, you were but a child, bouncing on your father's lap."

"Yes, well... out with the old, in with the new," he said, glancing at his Black Knights with a chuckle. "So, I am here, in your presence, as you requested, and yet your wizard's bubble is still up."

"In time, my Lord. But first, I wish to negotiate the terms of my surrender, for it is proper for kings to do so in circumstances such as this."

"Kings of old, perhaps, which I am not. I alone will now dictate what is proper." Pompeus surveyed the room. "Seems as if you've killed three of my men, and I only one of yours. That's a pretty good start for you, I would say. Why not come out and see how this thing plays out. Your luck may continue."

Bartkull said, "I have ordered the doors to my treasury

left open. Take what gold and silver you think is fair... and leave in peace."

"I think I deserve it all, and indeed it will be collected. But I seek something more valuable than gold and silver."

One of the urklings produced a satchel, loosened its string, and poured a small pile of some sort of powder into his hand. After an incantation, he spit into the powder and stirred it. For a moment the mixture burned like acid before twinkling and becoming airborne, wafting over to Quagley's bubble, penetrating it quite easily. The powder irritated the occupants of the bubble as if they'd inhaled a bit of guntspice, making them a little teary-eyed, but they were otherwise unaffected.

Pompeus continued. "Have you noticed that I chose not to bombard your castle with my catapults? For what pleasure would I draw from bombarding empty buildings? You may think it crafty of you to send your people away, but rest assured, I will make sport of hunting them down. I know they can't be far. Fires still smolder in their huts, and fresh dung lay along the horse paths.

"My Lord," said an urkling to Pompeus, "I observed that the pretty one smelled our burning flesh, which begged the question of how the scent entered the bubble. So, I conducted one more test. If my theory is correct, the wizard uses a bubble that merely repels minerals, metal, and magic, but with something organic it may have trouble."

"Really," Pompeus said with a grin, wheeling around to his Black Knights. "Knights, sever the head from atop a halberd. Sharpen the end. Fashion me a wooden spear."

The knights held one halberd to the floor, chopping off its metallic head with the axe of another. The knight that held the remaining wooden staff used a sword to shave the end to a point. He handed it to his king.

Pompeus made a show of slowly pushing the spear

through Quagley's bubble, which it penetrated without issue, jabbing into Bartkull's shoulder, not enough to harm him but enough to knock him back. The largest of grins grew across Pompeus' face.

Bartkull sighed, nodding to Quagley. The wizard lifted his staff from the floor. A spark arced between his staff and the floor just before the bubble slowly peeled away, from top to bottom.

Princess Vesponika tightened her grip around her father's waist, cowering fearfully. Bartkull's knights trembled, rattling their useless chainmail, for they knew their ends were at hand.

Bring that one here," Pompeus said, pointing to one of Bartkull's knights. A Black Knight, who was broad and towered over Bartkull's men, grabbed the poor knight, ripping him away from the others, flinging him onto the stone floor.

Bartkull's knight swung his sword at the Black Knight's leg, but the sword merely clanged off the black armor and slid away, not even inflicting a dent.

Pompeus used the tip of his wooden spear to nudge up the knight's chainmail with some finesse, then drove the tip of the spear into his abdomen, a wound that wasn't immediately mortal but caused him to scream wretchedly, writhing in pain.

Patherin reached out sympathetically to the knight, who was also a friend, and shed a tear. He turned spitefully to Pompeus, bellowing, "Murderer!"

"Yes, quite so." Pompeus said as his Black Knights seized their weapons, "And there are barely enough of you here to satisfy my insatiable appetite to snuff out life, but nevertheless, I will play around with your lives as a cat plays with a fluval before the kill. This will all end with your severed heads on pikes. But come, first regale me with this Theatrica Mechanica that I have heard so much about, that has somehow become renowned throughout the world, that despite all my vast accomplishments, is still held over my head that 'Your kingdom is grand, but Bartkull's kingdom contains the Theatrica Mechanica, the greatest wonder of the world.'" Pompeus said this last part in a shrill, mocking voice.

"The Theatrica Mechanica has been destroyed by fire," Bartkull bluffed, "just last week. I have a beautiful oil painting of it, if you wish."

"Lies," Pompeus screamed ragefully, swinging his bloody spear, striking Bartkull with a blunt blow to his temple, knocking off his crown, sending it skittering across the floor.

The blow dropped Bartkull to his knees, leaving Vesponika exposed. That's when Pompeus first took notice of her, looking her up and down.

Vesponika took refuge behind Quagley, Patherin, and the knights for a moment, but upon hearing her father's agonizing moans, she rushed to his side, trying in vain to help him to his knees.

"What's this? A sliver of beauty in this pitiful excuse for a castle?" Pompeus said, pulling her away from her father.

The silver knights moved to protect the King and princess but were quickly halted by the halberds and swords of the Black Knights.

"I want you to know that your father's foolishness has sealed your fate. Had he not sent his people away, I might have snatched you up, hidden you in the sanctuary of my harem, for you are almost as beautiful as the rumors. But beautiful women are plentiful in my kingdom, and I'm in a pinch here." He continued in a shrill laugh, "I need something to satisfy my troops, and you're the only morsel around."

Pompeus pushed her into the arms of one of the Black Knights. "Take her to the troops. Let them have their way. See to it she lasts. Bring me her head tomorrow."

Acting quickly to save Vesponika, Quagley pointed his staff toward Pompeus and said, "Emanessence to the one I gaze upon!"

A vapor left Quagley's staff, floating to Pompeus, gathering in the bowl of his black crown, soaking into his head.

Pompeus gave no indication of seeing the vapor, as his back had been turned to Quagley, but the urklings saw it and took quick retribution. Their eyes glassed over and an incantation left their lips in unison. Smoke black as tar formed within their palms for a moment, and then at once combined in the air and pounced on Quagley, engulfing him. Screaming was heard, but Quagley could not be seen from within an ever-shrinking black ball of smoke. The smoke paused its shrinking for a moment as Quagley's staff was spat from it, rattling onto the floor. Without the staff, the shrinking commenced at a quicker pace until it, and Quagley, were no more.

Vesponika had been kicking and screaming as a Black Knight dragged her by her hair from the great hall with two other knights close behind. They were nearly out the door when Pompeus yelled, "Stop!"

They stopped, turning toward Pompeus – their bulging, bloodshot eyes barely visible through the slats in their helmets.

"I have changed my mind. I will keep the girl."

"Lord Pompeus," one urkling said, standing before him and clasping his nubby hands. "The wizard has cast upon you a spell. An enamoring incantation of some variety. Give us but an hour to consult with the darkness and we will devise a counter-spell."

Pompeus gazed at Vesponika, who had been released and was laboring to her feet. "If it is a spell, I don't care. I will keep the girl for myself. I have spoken."

He turned to his knights. "Take her quickly; hide her from the troops. See to it that no harm comes to her."

The knight flung Vesponika over his shoulder. She pounded her fists on his clanky armor to no avail, for they all left in a hurry.

Feisty one, "Pompeus grinned as he watched her being carried out. The smile disappeared from his face as he turned to Bartkull and his shrinking entourage. "The Theatrica Mechanica! Where is it? That is what has led me here to plunder."

"I tell you, it is destroyed," Bartkull said.

One of Bartkull's silver knights glanced at the newly constructed wall, just for a moment, looking then as if he'd made a mistake.

An urkling, the observant one who'd figured out how to defeat Quagley's bubble, drifted to the wall, inspecting it closely. "Look, my Lord. The mortar in this wall is new. It is still wet in places."

King Pompeus went to the wall, gouging the mortar with a fingernail. "Yes, you are right; it is still soft." He sized up at the wall, which extended to the high ceiling. "Look how the timbers align. This is a false wall. Bring in workers to take it down. See to it they are careful."

Pompeus went to the knight he had stabbed and drove his spear into his face, visibly disappointed that the man had already expired. He ordered Bartkull, Patherin, and the remaining silver knights bound as his men dismantled the wall stone by stone. The task was easy as the mortar had barely set. Soon Pompeus was able to climb himself up the rubble and peek into the hidden room.

"Ah, and there it is, just like the rumors. It is enormous. Is it running as we speak? How wonderful. All the little things that move and turn within it. I have never seen something so magnificent!"

He turned to Bartkull. "You kept this... this object of indescribable majesty in your insignificant little kingdom all these years, and you let anyone who ever desired to experience it do so freely? You fool! Don't you understand what men will pay for such a wonder? Such entertainment? What made you think you were worthy of stewarding such a device? Once it is safely in my kingdom, men will sail across the great seas, coming from the farthest reaches of the four corners, offering up a month of wages to gaze upon this Theatrica Mechanica."

He stumbled back down the rubble, grabbing a foot soldier by the sleeve, "Summon the siegeworks engineers. Surely they will know how to move such an enormous thing. I'll bet it will require thirty oxen. Maybe more... yes. Send for fifty oxen, just in case.

As his men clattered and clanged their tools, dismantling the wall and conveying away the rubble, Pompeus turned to Bartkull. "Bartkull, your scheme is laughable! Did you really think I would not find your wonderful Theatrica Mechanica behind this hastily constructed wall? Did you think you could somehow keep it after your death?" He pulled himself up by the shoulder of one of his workers, sending the poor man tumbling down the rubble and to the floor, and climbed back up to look through a now larger hole. "The world-renowned Theatrica Mechanica is now mine, and *I* will make a place for it in my great hall. And what's this? You in there! Who are you? Come out of there at once!"

Lambert the Tinkerer emerged from the hole, crawling over the rubble, going to Pompeus with his head held low.

Pompeus looked him over, then scoffed to Bartkull, "You built your caretaker into the wall? This I did not expect from you. Why?"

"I could not risk him being killed," Bartkull said.

"I see. So this man is important to you? More important than even your princess? Perhaps I'll take pleasure in sawing off his head slowly as I watch defeat well up on your face."

"That is your choice, Pompeus, for I am in no position to bargain for Lambert the Tinkerer's life. But I think you underestimate the complexity of the Theatrica Mechanica that you so covet." He nodded towards Lambert. "Lambert is the creator of this device, and the only one in the world that can make it operate as it should. If you kill him, the Theatrica will quickly fall into disrepair. Truth be told, it will likely need much calibration after you transport it, and may even be completely inoperable upon arrival to your kingdom. Surely you would be mocked endlessly for lacking the resources to display your spoils in their full splendor."

Pompeus' men nearly had the wall deconstructed completely, enough so that he could now look see the Theatrica Mechanica in its entirety. "Yes, now that you mention it, it does look vastly more complex than anything I have ever laid eyes upon."

He turned to his men, clearing his throat. "I will have our tinkerers study this mechanism and learn it thoroughly. In the meantime, keep this Lambert fellow alive. Transport him back to the kingdom along with the Theatrica Mechanica. Once I am sure I don't need him anymore, I will make a show of his execution. Perhaps I will even have our tinkerers arrange for him to be executed by his very own device, upon the stage of its theater, by all these automatons I've heard so much about."

Pompeus sneered at Bartkull. "In the end, the Theatrica Mechanica is the only thing that will survive your kingdom."

* * *

Two Weeks Later

Lambert wiped sweat from his brow with the back of his greasy hand, rubbing it on his garment. Beyond a movable wall, he heard the chatter and smelled the wafting perfumes of people filling Pompeus' great hall. He nodded to Pompeus' servants, and they immediately began moving the panels one at a time, revealing the Theatrica Mechanica to many who had never laid eyes upon it (though by legend it was instantly recognizable to everyone).

They gasped and ooh'd, and in the end, applauded, praising Pompeus endlessly for conquering some meaningless kingdom up in the Seventh Realm that no doubt was never worthy of having such a brilliant and wonderous device. They failed to even regard Lambert, the grease-laden servant standing near the machine with oilcan in hand. They were oblivious to the fact that he was the one responsible for all this wonder.

The room was vastly larger than Bartkull's, with ceilings that soared to dizzying heights, lofty balconies, and towering windows of colored glass. Nevertheless, Pompeus's stonemasons had to partially demolish and re-construct a wall so his siegeworks engineers could move in the mighty Theatrica Mechanica. The ornate surroundings of its new home failed to diminish its breathtaking beauty, or the mysteriousness of its workings, although unlike Bartkull, King Pompeus left his throne in the place of highest honor and arranged the Theatrica off to the side, where his court would temporarily swivel their chairs to witness the chiming of the hours.

Until that day, Pompeus' two tinkerers hounded Lambert, peering over his shoulder endlessly as he programmed and tuned the Theatrica. At first, Lambert was vague in his instructions for calibrating pendulums, lubricating cogs, adjusting centrifugal regulators, and so on. But the more suspicious Pompeus' tinkerers became, the more forthcoming Lambert felt he had to be, carefully and deliberately giving the impression that he was withholding nothing. He realized it would take them years to master the machine, if that was even possible, and the more they came to recognize its complexity and report it to Pompeus, the greater the chance he would be kept alive to see the plan through.

But that morning, when they asked questions about a certain vessel deep inside the Theatrica, Lambert took quick action, rendering them both unconscious with blows to the head, hiding them in the blacksmith's keep deep in the castle's underground.

Lambert remained faithful to his slain king, and desperately wanted the devised plan to succeed. He never quite figured out why, years earlier, Quagley decided to lure a manticore into his cave, charm it with a spell, and then collect its gas-venom, also known in some realms as "creeping death". Only Lambert knew of the wizard's strange hobby, for he alone traveled to Quagley often, collecting vessels of his sparkle gasses and exploding powders for use in the Theatrica, and once, by chance, he heard the guttural moan of the beast held captive in the dark depths of that cave. Later, on a night when Quagley had a few too many mugs of grog, Lambert seized the opportunity, coaxing the wizard into divulging his purposes for keeping the beast.

Quagley had been refining and bottling the manticore's venom for years, for reasons Lambert never fully understood and – now that Quagley was dead – never would. But had it not been for the wizard's peculiar hobby, there would currently be no hope for the remnants of Bartkull's kingdom taking refuge in the mountains of Evermore. The Realm of Evermore was indeed a crafty place to hide, but Pompeus's resources were vast, his scouts plentiful and accustomed to long journeys into unknown lands, and given enough time Bartkull's people would eventually be found and slaughtered.

Lambert glanced furtively into a crowd of people larger than he'd ever seen gathered in one place. Pompeus had constructed additional seating for his great hall. His stone masons expanded the balconies. For his new Theatrica Mechanica's inaugural eruption, he would cram three thousand subjects into his throne room if he could. He took great pleasure flaunting the spoils of his conquests before his kingdom, and despite all the silver, gold, gems of all colors, slaves, wild beasts, and exotic weapons that he had accumulated over the years, the Theatrica Mechanica was to be his greatest possession.

Colorful tents had been set up within the castle's bailey and on the grounds surrounding the castle, each one carefully positioned so that even those not important enough to be invited into his hall and witness the eruption first-hand would be able to hear the music from within the tents. A festival had begun days ahead of the eruption – a well-festooned celebration where the subjects of the kingdom waited in procession to walk past a window that showed but a small portion of Theatrica Mechanica, whetting their appetites by revealing a portion of its vast complexity. People got lost for a moment in the mesmerizing cadence of its many swinging pendulums, steam purge pipes, and rolling marbles. Those whose place in line just happened to come near as the machine chimed the hours counted themselves lucky to see one of the many autonomous creatures folded under its stage get dispatched to somewhere they could not see.

Now the hour of the first eruption approached. The king's chief officers sorted the thousands, chasing out those who were only appointed to listen from the tents and verifying those who remained in the great hall were on the king's list. The Black Knights were stationed at all the entrances to the hall.

The king's advisors harked the bellmen in the castle's belfry. The ringing bells announced the king's entrance into his hall, prompting everyone to stand. Young girls entered first, sprinkling green leaves and laying stemmed flowers along the path the King would walk. The king's litter arrived outside the entrance, carried by eight strong servants. The litter was carefully set on the ground and the King stepped out, entering the hall with a proud grin.

Following the King were select women from Pompeus's harem, among them Princess Vesponika. Upon seeing her, Lambert's heart sank. He'd hoped not to see her there, in that way, having been stripped of her royal garments, forced to wear the dressings of a common servant. Her face was emaciated, her eyes downcast and her spirit broken.

Pompeus ascended the royal platform and surmounted his throne. Two Black Knights stood sentry behind him. Pompeus said a few words before directing everyone's attention to the Theatrica Mechanica.

The King summoned Lambert to the throne, pulling him

close by his collar, whispering, "Don't stand by your machine. You're not part of the show."

"Yes, my Lord."

"If your contraption fails to go off properly, I will have you strung up and slowly disemboweled as a substitute spectacle."

"Understood, my Lord."

He surveyed the room. "And where are *my* tinkerers?"

"I do not know, my Lord. They failed to appear this morning."

Pompeus eyed Lambert suspiciously. "Stay close," he said, shoving Lambert away. He summoned the two Black Knights forward. "My tinkerers are missing. Find them immediately."

The Knights left the hall in haste, beckoning more of their kind to follow. Lambert lingered atop the throne platform, surreptitiously making his way behind the harem, where Princess Vesponika was standing.

Vesponika was surprised when someone from behind took her hand, but when she turned and saw Lambert, joy washed over her face. She quickly turned back to avoid drawing attention, but she couldn't help a faint smile. She squeezed Lambert's hand lovingly, tilting her head, allowing him to whisper something into her ear.

"Swallow this potion the moment of the eruption, my princess." He placed a small vial carefully into her hand, closing her fingers tightly over it. "It is from Quagley, and will save your life."

"What will happen?" Vesponika whispered.

"You will see, my princess, very soon you will see."

A puff of steam and the clacking of cogs began from somewhere within the Theatrica Mechanica, drawing all eyes to it. Observers in the balconies focused their looking glasses on it, hoping to catch a closer glimpse of the mechanical wonders they've heard rumors of for so many years. Old women in white make-up fanned themselves. Important looking men of the king's court stroked their beards.

Small puffs of steam jetted here and there. Gears whirred to life. The Theatrica's cover retracted and its stage unfolded itself section by section, eliciting "oohs" and "ahs" from the crowd, followed by tumultuous applause.

A series of melodious bells rang out from the Theatrica, the prelude to the seventh hour. From a burrow within a field of false grass and metal twistwood trees whose branches swayed in a make-believe wind, the first automaton emerged in the form of a cute little marpet jaw. After a minute of searching the meadow for food, it scurried up one of the trees, finding a bundle of acorns. From atop the swaying branch, it dropped seven acorns and, as each one hit the artificial ground, a low-toned bell was struck, marking the seventh hour – the hour of the eruption.

With a great puff of steam and a speeding of the pendulums, the field of grasses and trees folded and retracted into the Theatrica as it transformed itself into a stage. An unseen orchestra of stringed and winded instruments began a concert. Everyone assumed it to be Pompeus's musicians off in another part of the castle, and wondered how the sound was transported so harmoniously to the great hall.

Princess Vesponika removed a tiny cork from a glass vial not even the size of her pinky and swiftly downed its contents.

From behind a purple curtain the first automaton emerged. The way it walked, mimicking human behavior so precisely, left the crowd breathless, for they had never seen such things, nor had they even dreamt of them. The way the automaton's mechanical eyebrows, cheeks, and lips conveyed human characteristics was uncanny.

The automaton was dressed in the purple colors of King Pompeus, and the black crown upon its head was a close replica, leaving no doubt it was meant to represent the king. Pompeus himself showed surprise to see his likeness on the half-scale stage.

As the Theatrica's curtain lifted, the crowd gasped, realizing the orchestra they had been hearing was actually about a hundred automatons at the rear of the Theatrica Mechanica's stage.

A castle large enough for children to play in slid to the forefront of the stage. The orchestra changed to a rhythmic, marching melody. The automatous king drew a sword as knights and foot soldiers joined him, marching toward the castle in rhythm with the orchestra's drums.

Lambert's attention was drawn away from his Theatrica. To his horror, he watched the Black Knights return with Pompeus's tinkerers. He never thought they'd been found so quickly.

The tinkerers pointed accusing fingers across the voluminous room, directly at Lambert, drawing the attention of a few in the crowd.

At that very moment, on the Theatrica's stage from somewhere behind the orchestra, a mechanical head on a pike appeared. A body for the head rose up out of a trap door in the stage, meant to be a grave. The body was clothed in red and blue, with Bartkull's signature yellow insignia. It snatched the head from the pike and attached it to its shoulders. Then it seized the pike, thrusting it into the king. A show was then made of the automatous version of King Pompeus' death.

At this, the crowd began to grumble. Some even dared to chuckle. From atop one of the balconies echoed an amused guffaw.

The real King Pompeus lurched to his feet. "Stop this contraption at once!"

Pompeus's tinkerers ran to the machine, opening its covers, working frantically to stop it. With puffs of steam, all of the stage's lanterns were extinguished. A loud whirring noise brought the pendulums to a standstill, the automatons froze in position and the music ground to a halt.

The Black Knights tore through the crowd, seizing Lambert, dragging him before the king.

Pompeus's face burned with rage. Before he could open his mouth, no doubt to pronounce swift judgment on Lambert's life, a loud, decisive thud drew his attention.

The thud came from within the Theatrica Mechanica. It shook the floor and rattled dust from the rafters. Even the fabric of the tents just outside the entrances vibrated.

A shrill hissing was heard next.

From within the Theatrica Mechanica, green gas poured out, the leading edges of which were billows that took on the forms of charging manticores. The green gas surged off in every direction. Those in the great hall panicked. Women shrieked. Men screamed in fear.

In an instant, the air was turned green. Everyone surged for the exits. None made it, for creeping death works quickly to paralyze its victims before slowly killing them.

Pompeus dropped like a sack of beans, leaving him gagging on the floor, trying to figure out what happened. The Black Knights dropped just after. Lambert held his breath, which afforded him but a few moments to watch Pompeus's kingdom fall before easing himself to the floor.

Lambert heard the screams of thousands in the tents as they, too, were surely being annihilated, for the manticore's creeping death is renowned for its ability to wipe out entire villages.

In the confusion of fallen, twitching bodies, Princess Vesponika found Lambert the Tinkerer on the floor, close to the throne. "Lambert, did you not swallow your potion?"

Lambert looked on as the veins in his forearm turned black. He turned to Vesponika, doing his best to put on a smile and mumbling weakly, "Remember, you weren't supposed to be here. There was but one vial, my princess. It took Quagley years to collect the manticore's gas-venom, and years more of failed counterpotions to finally perfect one that might work." He caressed her cheek. "And work it has."

"But, you'll die now. Could we not have split the potion in half?"

"It wasn't worth the risk. I am old, my child. You have your whole life ahead of you, and a kingdom to run. You must go to our people in the mountains of Evermore. Tell them everything that has been done. You will be made queen."

The green gas lifted, but the creeping death had done its part. The people of Pompeus's kingdom littered the floor, moaning in agony. Some had already expired.

Vesponika's tears flowed for Quagley. She pulled him close, hugging him, kissing him on the cheek.

"I die soon," Lambert whispered in her ear. "I consider you my daughter. My Theatrica Mechanica has always brought you joy. You almost know how to make it run, and you will figure out the rest. See to it that it is brought back to your father's kingdom."

"I will, Lambert. I promise."

Vesponika returned Lambert gently to the floor.

He watched her stand and walk over to Pompeus. She snatched her father's sword from his grasp, with its ruby red jewel glimmering in the hilt. Pompeus held up a weak, shaking hand to Vesponika, which did nothing to help him as she drove the blade through both his hand and his chest.

Lambert turned his head, looking over his Theatrica Mechanica proudly before his eyes closed for the last time.

What If?

by Debra Robic

Have you ever wondered – I'm sure you have, hasn't everyone? – how different your life would be if you had made a different choice somewhere in your past? Chosen a different spouse, a different school, a different career? Decided to marry, or not? Decided to meet that coworker for drinks after work, or not? Decided to have a family? Or not?

I often find myself looking around this room, to the extent that my stiff, creaky neck will allow me to do so, at the bland beige walls, hung here and there with washed out watercolor prints of vague settings, wondering what fork in the road brought me to this benign internment. Of course, a part of it is just living so long – in my case, some 75 years, so far. Being this old, of course, qualified me for a placement in the State Senior Living Facility, where they take care of my every need – every meal, every medical procedure, every entertainment. In fact, it was mandated that I be so housed, beginning on my 70th birthday. Well, I'm not telling you anything you don't know – seven decades of productive life being considered optimal, there are no free-range elderly folks anymore. Too likely for them – I mean us – to hurt ourselves, be unable to care for ourselves, become a burden on society. Here, in the SSLF, we are contained, protected, and managed, at a minimal cost to those who are still youthful and therefore still useful.

Now and again, I regard myself in the small mirror hung on the faded pink wall above my bathroom sink, lighted by the single-bulb fixture directly above. I say I regard myself in this mirror – but in my mind, the image that stares back at me is a stranger. I'm the first to admit that I was not just a little vain in my younger years, fighting age by dying my hair to maintain my natural dark brunette color, judiciously applying make-up to hide the wrinkles and age spots and maintain what I hoped was a natural rosy glow of cheeks and lips, and most importantly, taking arms against becoming *old* by the application of all the attitude I could muster. Did pretty well, too. Most people had no idea I was anywhere near my actual age.

Except the State. For them, it was a matter of record, associated with my identity chip, numbered and logged along with millions of others since chip insertion was first mandated under the National Identity Protection Initiative, passed in 2023.

So it was that precisely on my 70th birthday, December 14th, 2040, State agents arrived at the door of my home, and handed me a copy of my Elder Removal Warrant – a mere formality, really, a holdover from the old due-process days, as my Removal was federal law as soon as I hit the magic seven-0. I have since had time to marvel at the improvement in the State's efficiency in handling such administrative business; it has seemed to increase in direct inverse proportion to the removal of individual freedoms — things we used to call "rights." Inalienable, my ass.

The Agents who arrived for my Removal were indistinguishable from one another, indeterminately young, beardless, hair slicked back from their foreheads and pulled into neat buns at the napes of their necks, dressed in identical black pants and white tunics that made them look like dentists, to me. I couldn't be sure whether they were male or female, and knew better than to ask or signal any uncertainty by a misplaced pronoun.

"I'm sorry," I dithered, looking at the Warrant as if it mattered. "I- I'm not quite ready. I haven't packed." I hated how tremulous my voice sounded. At the same time, I hoped it would win me some consideration.

"You don't need to pack," one of the Agents said. Its voice was as genderless as its features. "Under the Equitable Eldercare Act of 2025, all residents of State Senior Living Facilities are provided with everything needed for everyday life for the duration of their Care Term."

It went without saying that the duration of a senior's Care Term was the rest of their life. I tried not to give any thought to the conspiracy theorists' rumors that the State had applied a very specific "Use By" date to the term of elder incarceration, and if citizens weren't civic-minded enough to die on their own by that time, well, there were means to ensure the availability of space for the next batch of septuagenarians. Don't ask me how I got wind of such rumors; if the State doesn't know, I'd like to keep it that way – I don't want my expiration date coming any sooner than necessary. It doesn't matter now, anyway. Elders (how I hate that word!) under the State's "care" have no access to outside sources of information. Small distinction, since even those not yet "aged out" of society have precious little access to real information, either.

In any case – or as it happens in every case – I was gently but firmly helped into the Elder Removal Van with nothing but the clothes on my back, and my copy of the Warrant. That would have been worth the paper it was printed on (a quaint nod to the olden days), if I had had a pen and could have used the blank back of the page to have written something meaningful. Maybe a note saying, *Help! I have been abducted by androgynous goons with nefarious intentions!* Sadly, as for all elders going through Removal, there was no one to appeal to, anyway. Besides, I expect the idea of providing a writing implement had been discussed and discarded, as it was just such nonsense that enabled the writing of that insurrectionist document, the erstwhile Constitution of the United States. Now *that* was a document worth the parchment it had been written on.

So here I am, five years later, standing in front of my merciless State-issued mirror, hair chopped short and fully gray, barefaced, dressed in baggy navy sweats (I have my choice of navy, olive green, or brown; I mix it up) and slip-on sneakers, staring at an image that absolutely cannot have any relationship to *me*. And yes, this is one of those times I wonder what choice, what turning point in life's road did I take that brought me here, turning me into this drab, lifeless husk, so completely hiding the intelligence, love of humor, and curiosity about life that was still *me*. The real me. The one that had never been reflected by this miserable little mirror.

My apartment – my cell, really – is on the third floor of the SSLF, its dark door halfway down a long hall of such doors, distinguishable only by the number 333 printed on the white plastic plate affixed to it. The nondescript door opens into a room that is in every particular like a hotel room, serving as both bedroom and sitting area. Unlike a decent hotel room, there is no kitchenette, no microwave, just a mini fridge. All meals are taken at specifically scheduled times in the common room on the first floor, and no food is allowed in the residents' rooms. The one window is opposite the door, and looks out over the employee vehicle charging lot; residents are not allowed vehicles, which is fine, because our driving privileges are revoked at the time of Elder Removal anyway. Directly across the charging lot is an identical SSLF. I have never seen anyone standing in any of those windows looking back at our building, but then, there is nothing here worth looking at.

To the left as you enter the room is the bathroom, which features a hospital green-tiled shower stall, complete with sturdy safety bars and a built-in tiled seat, on which I cannot bring myself to place my naked bottom – the rooms are cleaned by housekeeping staff during residents' assigned time in the dining hall, so I have never seen it done. Call me paranoid – or stubborn – but I shower standing, as I have done all my life. It's a small and insignificant act of rebellion, but you take what you can get.

Next to the shower stall is a small sink. Between the sink and shower stall is a toilet, with a little shelf above it to hold incidentals – like toothpaste, soap, and prescription pill bottles. Lots of prescription pill bottles, all provided free of charge by the State Social Medicine Agency. They are each deemed necessary to keep something down – blood pressure, cholesterol, blood sugar, acid reflux... I suspect even the residents, themselves. I flush mine down the toilet, one of these in the morning after breakfast, two of these midday, one of those before bedtime, and carefully avoid eating the cafeteria foods (most of what is served) that I know to be harmful to my health. So far, I have sailed through my obligatory State Care Officer's visits with the same results: "Your test results look fine. I'm just going to go ahead and order refills on your prescriptions so we can keep everything in line."

So this is my life, day in and day out. The only bright spot is Alan, my next-door neighbor in #332. Like me, he has been steadfastly recalcitrant throughout his incarceration. At least as much as possible; I suspect he might be a stand-up bather, as well, although we've never discussed it. But we do talk whenever we can – which is mostly during our scheduled mealtimes. Residents are not allowed to fraternize, otherwise; no visitors allowed in our rooms, even other residents. And the only times we're allowed to leave our rooms are for scheduled activities – meals, exercise yard, movie nights – for our safety, of course. When the tone sounds signaling that we are to make our way down to the dining hall, we wait for one another in the hall outside of our doors, looking forward to our brief opportunity for human interaction.

"Morning, Trip," he greets me. Alan's nickname for me, derived from the triple threes of my room number. As usual, his wispy gray hair stands up every which-way, making it look like he just rolled his lanky frame straight out of bed and out the door.

But his eyes were bright, as was his mind, and he had a wit so sharp that its victims rarely felt the cut.

"Hello, Deuce," I reply, since he is 33-two. We think we are very clever. "What's new this morning?"

Alan smiles broadly, eyes full of mischief, and instead of his usual "What could be new?", he catches me off guard with, "I got a wonderful new book from the library."

Surprised, I look at him, eyebrows raised, waiting for an explanation. The SSLF "library" is a small bookshelf located in the common room where we gather for meals. And for movie nights, if you can stomach a steady diet of State-produced propaganda films. The several dozen books on the bookshelf are similarly curated, old classics that no one really wants to read, nature books about the migratory habits of Emperor penguins or the grooming practices of kangaroos and other marsupials, or superficial travel guides that have been out of date for decades. The idea that Alan had found a "wonderful new book" among this second-hand literary detritus was inconceivable.

"I did," he assured me, raising his right hand slightly to show me that he did, indeed, carry a small book, with what looked like a red leather cover. It was the size of what we used to call pocketbooks.

Down in the dining hall, we picked a spot as far from other diners as possible, made sure no staff were lurking nearby, and Alan passed the book to me under the table. Taking a cue from his caution, I surreptitiously tucked it under the elastic waistband of my sweatpants, safely hidden under my bulky oversized sweatshirt.

"Okay, Deucey, what gives?" I asked, leaning in close and keeping my voice low.

"I'm not kidding," he said. "I actually found it here in the library. I was so bored and desperate, I decided to see if there was anything here I could make myself read, or reread, and tucked between *Sense and Sensibility* and *Victory* was that little gem."

"Why the cloak-and-dagger? Why not just tell me, and let me check it out?"

"Because I don't think it was supposed to be there," he said quietly.

I sat for a moment with that thought. Something out of State control in the perfectly ordered SSLF? That was something I had not seen in my five years as a resident. That was different. Like Bill Murray in *Groundhog Day* I thought, *anything different is good.*

"Racy romance? Copy of the founding documents? What?"

Alan continued without looking up, doing his best to appear completely absorbed by the task of chasing errant peas around his plate with a fork. I had to strain to hear him. "No nothing like that, but I'm sure if they knew of its existence it wouldn't be here."

"Why is that?"

"Because it asks questions, he replied. "Well, a very specific question. It's titled *What If?*"

"Sounds pretty benign."

He grinned, then popped the last of the peas into his mouth. "You'll see," he said when he had finished chewing. He pointed to the mound of peas still on my plate. "You going to eat those?"

I shook my head and pushed my plate over so he could scoop my leftovers onto his plate.

"Just wait till you read it," he said. "Then let me know what you think."

I nodded, and retrieved my plate, appearing to take an interest in the untouched glob of instant mashed potatoes, as I spotted an approaching staff member. I had taken to calling all of them *Big Nurse* in my mind.

"Eat up now, Ms. Winters," she admonished me, seeing my mostly untouched plate. I had forced myself to eat the gristly Salisbury steak patty, but had no intention of choking down the lump of "potatoes," and would absolutely not touch the soggy roll that sat in a pool of greasy gravy run-off from the steak patty.

"Oh, yes, I am," I chirped in my best little-old-lady voice. "Have to take it a bit slowly these days, though. Aggravates my reflux, otherwise!" I didn't have reflux – precisely because I didn't eat the massive amount of empty carbs that were part of our carefully balanced diet, straight out of the State Nutrition Guide. I belched elaborately, for emphasis.

Big Nurse winced, noted that Alan (who was trying hard to conceal his mirth) appeared to be busily chasing down peas, and moved on. What a life. What a farce.

What If? I felt the small book pressed against my abdomen under my shirt. It seemed to have grown warm, and suddenly I couldn't wait to get back to my room to read it.

* * *

What If?
The Pliable Possibility of the Past

The poet Robert Frost wrote:

"I shall be telling this with a sigh
Somewhere ages and ages hence:
Two roads diverged in a wood, and I—
I took the one less traveled by,
And that has made all the difference."

Perhaps you have read the poem, "The Road Not Taken," that these lines are from. And perhaps you wondered how the poet knew that, years later, he would look back on his decision in

162

the woods that day, and sigh, and know that down the road he had not taken lay something entirely different. What are we to make of that difference? As he contemplated it, did he sigh from disappointment? From weariness? From regret?

If you have traveled the roads of this world for more than a few decades, you may recognize the feeling, the reasons for your own sighs, as you look back on your own route. But you will likely turn away from such thoughts, as who could know whether taking one road or another would really make "all the difference"?

*For example, **what if** that pregnancy test you took with a sinking heart and shaking hands when you were sixteen had been negative, instead of positive? How different would your life have been?*

I slapped the little red book closed and tossed it to the foot of the State-issued, chenille-covered twin bed where I had propped myself up to read. My heart ran like a rabbit in my chest.

Don't be an idiot, I scolded myself. *That's just an example – a very common occurrence, teenage pregnancies. Nothing to do with your situation.* Even though I had been sixteen.

I got up and went into the bathroom to splash some cold water on my face, then patted it dry with this week's State-issued thin white hand towel. Actually, it was identical to last week's thin white hand towel, but presumably washed when new linens were delivered by one of the SSLF Comfort Unit workers each Monday morning. These worthies were every bit as amicable as the Big Nurse types in the dining room. In fact, they were, as far as I could tell, pretty much interchangeable. Except these I labeled

"Matron" (only in my head, of course). I pulled the scrap of towel away from my face and looked into the mirror.

I had gotten used to seeing a stranger in this miserable little looking glass, but not this stranger. Now, instead of someone impossibly old and dowdy, I saw a young girl – far younger than any reflection I had seen for many decades. She had round cheeks that wouldn't lean out for many years, making her look even younger than she was, and her dark eyes were red from crying. She looked down, presumably at her hands, and I at mine. When I lifted the small towel in my hands and looked up at my young reflection, she was holding up a pregnancy test strip, and the plus sign showed positive, even in an impossible backwards reflection.

I raised the towel and scrubbed furiously at my eyes for several seconds, then lowered and peeked over it slowly, to see... an old woman, gray-haired, saggy-skinned, and scared.

It took me a good hour until I was ready to pick up the book again. By that time I had convinced myself that I was just seeing things, that I had let my imagination run away with me. Understandable. I was so bored living the safe life in the SSLF that I was ready to run away – with my imagination, with a good book, with an old lover, more's the pity.

I picked up the little red-bound volume and opened to the place I had stopped reading. I reread the final paragraph:

> *For example, **what if** that pregnancy test you took with a sinking heart and shaking hands when you were sixteen had been negative, instead of positive? How different would your life have been?*

I had let myself think about it a bit. In my case – if this were to be considered my case – I had come to the conclusion that very little would have been different. Without the knowledge of my family or the potential teenaged father, all evidence of my transgression was quietly and efficiently removed at a very accommodating and easily accessible Planned Parenthood facility. When the procedure was finished, all that was left behind was a burden of private shame that I carried to term and years beyond, and shared with no one. Ever. I read on:

> *Now, you may think that things would not have been that different, really. If you hadn't been pregnant, you wouldn't have had to make, and live with, any hard decisions... other than whether or not to have unprotected sex in the future. But that was not the road you were on, was it? For you, the test was positive, and you did have to make that hard, heartbreaking decision.*

> **What if** *that has made all the difference?*

The book-brain barrier was breaking down with every sentence I read. I was no longer reading the words of an author who wrote, worked with an editor, published, went to book signings, and talked about the philosophical meaning of the characters' lives and situations. I was the author and the main character, and the situations were mine, and I desperately, desperately wanted an anonymous editor to strike that last line, with a note, *"Not sure how this moves the story forward. Wasn't this situation already resolved earlier in the story?"* I read on:

> *Here is your story, the way you chose:*

> *You are sixteen, you are pregnant. Everyone around you – teachers, friends, celebrities, politicians, doctors – all are very open-minded and*

supportive about young women like you making the choice not to complete an unwanted pregnancy. In harder terms, to get an abortion. In the harshest, but most honest of terms, to kill the life that has begun to grow within you.

"It is your body," they say.

"No one can force you to do anything you don't want to do with your body," they say.

"It would mean the end of your education, the end of your career aspirations. No one would blame you," they say.

"It won't cost you anything, and no one ever needs to know," they say.

So you chose their way, the "easy" way. How could you have known that killing the baby you carried, the person she might have been in the world, would also kill the person YOU were meant to be?

My face was wet with silent tears. This was ridiculous. I must have fallen asleep, and I was dreaming. I willed it to be so, letting the book fall to the floor and burying my face in my pitiful lump of a pillow. Eventually, I must have slept... or I was right, and I had just been dreaming the whole thing.

The next morning at breakfast I tried to give the book back to Alan under the table, but he held his hands up and refused to take it from me.

"Put it away," he hissed, glancing around to make sure no

Big Nurse was nearby.

"No! I don't want it!" I retorted. "It's weird! It must have really seemed weird to you, reading about some pregnant teenage girl! Why did you give it to me?"

The look on his face was a mixture of amusement and sympathy, which made me want to slap him. That'd bring staff running for sure!

"It did seem weird to me, at first, but not for the reason you think," Alan said quietly, still pretending to eat. "That wasn't my story."

"What do you mean?"

"What you're describing – that's not what I read."

I was thoroughly confused now. "What, you didn't start at the beginning? Why didn't you tell me there was some trick to reading it?"

Alan burst out in a guffaw that he had to quickly disguise as a coughing fit, as it drew the attention of a lurking Big Nurse.

I patted him on the back – maybe a little harder than our ruse demanded – and assured the attendant, "He's okay, just choked. I don't think the powdered eggs were sufficiently moistened this morning, my dear. Tell Cook, would you?" I gave her a smile dripping with every bit of saccharine I could muster. She gave me a look that could pickle an egg, even powdered.

"You are going to get us in big trouble, Deuce!" I whispered as I sat back down.

He shook his head, wiping his streaming eyes and trying to catch his breath. "Oh no, Trip! I'm going to set us free!"

"You're crazy, old man."

"Crazy like a fox, old lady!" he replied with a grin.

I rolled my eyes. "So how am I supposed to read this stupid book, then?" I said.

"Just like any other book," he replied. "You open the cover, start at the beginning, and turn the pages, reading them one by one."

I regarded him for several seconds. "What if... I can't?" I waited for him to laugh again, but he was serious for the first time since we sat down.

"You can. I know enough about you to know that. I know it will be hard. Wasn't easy for me either, even though my 'what ifs' are different. But I know you can do it, and I know you need to. Now don't ask me any more. Just read it." He reached across the table and covered my hand with his, giving it a little squeeze.

* * *

Back in my room, with a breakfast of powdered eggs and tofurkey bacon sitting like a lump in my stomach, I made myself pick up the book and continue reading where I had left off.

> *So with the voices of others – others, who did not bear the burden of your choice; others who would be gone in a moment – with those adamant, righteous voices crowding your ears, you made your choice. And you changed the future. Now you live in the world you created with that choice.*

I looked around me at the bland, close walls of my cell. I stood up, book in hand, and stepped over to my cheerless window. Was it truly a window that looked out onto a world I had created? How could that be? How would I choose to live in a world of such drab sameness, a world peopled with automatons, homogenous, hopeless, closed? I stood for long minutes, searching the limited view for answers, but the empty windows of the building on the other side of the charging lot simply stared back at me blankly; behind each window, I knew, was another inmate, fellow victim of Elder Removal. How could any personal choice of mine have resulted in this bleak world? Finally, I moved back to my bed, propped myself up against the pillows and, reluctantly, read on.

> *Now let us look at a different version of your story. Let us say that in this version, you somehow knew that you could not, must not, terminate your pregnancy. Let us say that you had a visit from a wise old woman, or an angel, perhaps – someone you trusted implicitly – who told you to hold on to the possibility of the life growing within you.* **What if** *you were so moved, so overcome, by her words, that you decided then and there to carry and give birth to the new life within you?*

> *You could have, you know. So, what would your life as a teenage mother have looked like?*

> *Pretty much exactly as you imagined it at the time: hard, heartbreaking, exhausting. Finishing high school would have been a struggle. Your family and friends, with one or two exceptions, would have been ashamed, offering little or no support – financial or emotional. Pursuing higher education would have been out of reach. Finding the energy to work full time and then some, and still be a good mother every day, would have seemed impossible. Yet you would have persevered.*

Yeah, right, I thought. I'd have been a freaking saint. I remembered the scared girl I had been – the round-cheeked, red-eyed face that had so recently appeared to stare back at me from my mirror – and I doubted she could have found the strength to fight the forces that swept her... that swept *me* up in a current of expediency and evasion, and landed me on the shore of despair that followed my actual decision.

And yet... I chewed absently on my thumbnail (a habit I shared with the younger me) and found myself thinking that maybe I underestimated myself. After all, down deep wasn't I the same person that I am now? I like to think I'm a smart, strong, self-reliant woman. Of course, I didn't think of myself that way then. How could I? The girl me standing in the pink-tiled bathroom in our small-town tract house, staring at the plus sign on that stick, was overwhelmed with fear and shame. All the voices in my head, in my life, in my world, were telling me to be smart for a change, take care of it, get on with my life and don't look back.

I smacked the book closed. It didn't do any good playing this what-if game. I did what I did.

And besides, this was just a book. Something someone wrote, a story similar to mine. Those similarities just brought up old hurts, and I had no need to revisit those. I made up my mind. Tucking the offending tome under my sweatshirt, I stepped out into the hall, relieved to see that it was empty. We still had another hour until our lunch shift, and the usually ubiquitous hall monitor Matron was nowhere to be seen. That was very good, because visiting between residents outside of lunch and exercise periods was vigorously discouraged by those goons.

I stepped quickly up to the door of #332 and tapped lightly. The door opened immediately, and I almost squealed as Alan grabbed my hand and pulled me into his room, glancing quickly up and down the hall before closing the door.

"Wow! If I'd known you'd be this happy to see me, I'd have stopped by sooner!" I teased, momentarily forgetting that I was here to give him his book and a piece of my mind.

He smiled, and that softened his reply some. "To be honest, my eagerness was more fear of discovery than delight in seeing you. Although I am delighted to see you, even if you have come loaded for bear." He stuck his hand out, palm up, waiting. It took me a minute to realize he was waiting for me to put the book in it.

I felt my cheeks flush as I pulled it out from under my shirt and put it in his hand. Now that I was here, I felt foolish. *Here's your book back. I don't like it. It scares me.* I tried to put a better face on it.

"Sorry," I said, "I just couldn't get into it." Sounded lame even to me.

"Uh-huh." He set the book on his "kitchen" table – same mini-dinette version as in my room, flanked by two small vinyl-covered chairs. They were all the same. "Anyway, I'd hate to think you came all this way for nothing. Have a seat – I think I have a can of O.J. in my fridge, if you're interested. And a pack of *petit beurre* cookies, if you like those."

I didn't ask where he scored the cookies. I was aware there was some sort of a black market among the inmates, but I had never participated. I wasn't even sure how it worked.

"I'll have a juice, thanks," I said, taking a seat. "That by itself should be sufficient to raise my blood sugar sky high without adding cookies. Though I have to admit, it's been a long time since I had *petit beurre*, and I'm very tempted."

"Aw, what the hell, live it up!" he laughed. "What're you worried about, anyway? Got a skinny little cocktail dress you want to be buried in?"

I laughed and accepted the juice and a cookie, in spite of myself. It occurred to me that I ought to sneak over here more often. Then it occurred to me that I wasn't likely to get away with it often. And that made me sad, and reminded me of why I was here.

"Do you ever think about what happened to us, Deuce? To our world, I mean."

He sat down across the tiny table and opened his can of juice. "I do," he answered, and took a sip before he added, "Especially lately."

"Why lately?"

His glanced at the red book lying on the table between us. "I've been doing some reading."

He looked up, and his frank gaze challenged me to tell the truth. And maybe more, to admit my fear.

"Look," I said, "I started reading about the young pregnant girl, and it struck a nerve. Too close to home, I guess."

"I told you at breakfast, that's not the story I read," he replied. "I read the story of Peter, the disciple."

"What? The bible story? I didn't see that in there." I thought maybe I hadn't read far enough. But I couldn't imagine the book I was reading suddenly veering off into a bible story.

"Well, you wouldn't." I don't know if it was his smirk or his words, but I suddenly wanted to dump the rest of my juice over his head.

"You wouldn't have read the story of Peter, because it wasn't your story," he continued. "It was mine. Not literally, of course. I was not hanging around with Jesus two-thousand years ago. But I did deny a good man, a good friend, when he needed me, because I was scared. Just like Peter. And my friend died, and part of me died with him, because I was ashamed that I was so busy covering my ass that I didn't do anything to help him when I could have. I made a choice out of fear and weakness, and I have had to live with the shame of that choice ever since. Sound familiar at all?"

I started to make a smartass remark, but I suddenly realized that Alan and I had been reading the same book, after all. A choice made out of fear, of weakness, and the life-changing shame of that choice. But maybe, even more than that.

I set my juice down and ran my fingers and thumbs

around the bottom of the can. It was cool and wet with condensation, normal and expected, and I savored the sensation for a moment. My mind was full of questions, but one was louder than all the others. "Did we do this, Alan? Is it possible that we made this screwed up world? I mean, us personally?"

"I don't have all the answers, Trip, but I think that is what the book is telling us," he said gently. "That we do change things with our choices, some of us. Not every one, not every choice, but key choices. Keys – literally – that lock or unlock pathways at critical junctures."

I leaned back in the chair and stretched my arms over my head, bringing them down with my fingers laced behind my head. I blew out a sharp breath. "Wow. We definitely did not read the same book, my friend. Mine didn't have any quantum physics, spooky action at a distance, or parallel universes in it!"

"Didn't it?" He raised one eyebrow and tilted his head. Reminded me of Spock from the old TV series.

I opened my mouth to answer, then clamped it shut, as I realized that Frost's story of two divergent roads, different outcomes beyond simply a changed route, were a pretty good layman's view of a parallel universe theory. I dropped my hands into my lap.

"Okay," I said. "Maybe you're right. But how does one person's choice – or even a few people's choices – change everything for everyone?"

Alan grinned, digging a couple more cookies out of the package and handing one to me. "Well, if you didn't like quantum physics, you're certainly not going to want to go on this next E-ticket ride into chaos theory and the butterfly effect."

"Stop!" I cried, throwing my hands in front of me, palms out – well, one palm out; I still held a cookie in the other, so it somewhat hampered the effect. "Okay, I'm layman-level familiar with that one. But how do we know what choices are these key choices? I mean, we're just going along living our lives - like the butterfly flapping its wings. Which flap causes the iceberg to rise up in the path of the Titanic? I mean, we can only trace the impact of any choice backwards in time, from effect to cause. And by then, it's too late."

"That, my dear, is where the hated book comes in," he patted the book on the table, in the process sliding it nearer to me. "If you will just read a little further."

I felt my lip curl into a sneer, but reluctantly grabbed the book anyway, and shoved it back under my shirt as I got up and headed for the door. I turned before I opened it, waved my cookie at him like a warning weapon and said, "The next time you want me to face my failings to save the sorry world, Deucey, just say so. And the next time you recommend a book, it had better be freaking Scheherazade and the Thousand and One Nights-level literature, you got me?"

He laughed - a sound that went a long way toward bolstering my courage to continue the quest, whatever it was. "No promises," he said, "but here's hoping for a happy ending, at least."

* * *

With a quick glance up and down the hallway to make sure no Matrons were nearby, I quickly slipped back into my room (indistinguishable from #332, except it lacked the conversation and snacks), and made myself open the book. As it had every time before, it opened right where I had left off. Unfortunately, that was the least inexplicable thing about it. Where was I? Oh, yeah, reading the dreary prospects I would have enjoyed as a single teenage mother. Really, how was that supposed to make me rethink my original choice? I took a deep breath, and read on:

It is hard to imagine the life you might have lived.
Much easier to remember *the life you did have.*

So let us stay with memory for a time.

Remember when, four years after your fateful de-cision, you dropped out of college to get married, taking on a ready-made family of stepchildren? Remember that you got no support from your family or friends when you made this decision? Now, remember as a young woman, working full time, struggling to make ends meet, to be a good mother to someone else's children, to be a good wife? Sounds hard. But you did it.

Remember later, when you went through getting divorced, being out of work, and having no place to live, all at the same time? Remember how you found a new job, and a small apartment within walking distance to work, since you didn't have a car. Remember hocking your wedding ring to get money for food – and getting $10, a dollar for each year you were married?

Yes, I remembered it. I hadn't thought about it for such a long time, it felt like remembering a movie, but it was definitely my life. Seeing it here, on the pages of this confounded book, I realized something about the female lead... she didn't make great decisions, but she stuck it out, she made it, she persevered. With a weird sense of dislocation, I corrected myself – *I* persevered. Reading this surreal version of *"This is Your Life,"* I began to see myself – or, more accurately, remember myself – in a new light. Behind the fear, under the shame and uncertainty, I saw strength. Maybe I could have borne it. Maybe I could have done it, after all.

And then I thought back to my conversation with Alan.

Perhaps this is the key to working backwards from outcome to inception, developing the knowledge that you have within you the power to have done what seemed, at the time, impossible. I felt the questions filling my mind, climbing one on top of another, and forced my attention back to the printed page:

> *Now let us shift from remembering to imagining. This is active imagining, like switching a train from one track to another. This is going back to the place two roads diverged, and envisioning, as if in a memory, taking a step down the road not taken.*
>
> *Envision yourself seeing the dreaded plus sign on the home pregnancy test. You will remember the fear, for that is real on either path. Go ahead and remember, too, the clamor of judgmental voices in your mind, telling you what to do. It is important to remember these immutable things, because you will need all your strength to overcome them.*
>
> *Remember looking up at the frightened young woman in the mirror, but this time, look deeply into her eyes... they hold something you must help her find within herself, because you are only able to see it from here, from this world, from this side of divergent choices.*
>
> *In this imagined past, you must guide her to take, as if she had done so already, a different path than the one you remember taking.*

*And don't be afraid that you don't have the
strength, the ability, to change her history. You
do, you always have had the strength. Now, you
must find the* will.

I felt like Dorothy standing outside the Emerald City,
hearing from Glinda that I had always had to power to go back.
Really? All I had been through, all I had lost, all the ugliness that,
apparently, I had created in this world... I could go back, just like
that?

I looked down at my State-issued knock-off trainers
(probably made by some poor kid in China). They were as far
from ruby slippers as you could get, and I could feel reality seep-
ing up from them, climbing my calves, above my waist and up to
my chin. Like icy water, it robbed me of strength, robbed me of
the ability to believe in the power of the book, or even in myself.

I pulled in a deep, panicky breath, and hugged the book
to my chest. I kicked my feet impatiently, as if trying to swim to
the surface, to escape the dark waters of fear before they could
drown me entirely. *I want to go home, I want to go home!* The
thought echoed over and over in my mind as I scuffed my feet
against the threadbare carpet of my room.

I stopped suddenly and forced myself to look around me.
No Emerald City. No ruby slippers. No dark waters. And in that
moment, I saw it all for what it was: an *illusion* of helplessness.
The very illusion that held this ugly world together, kept us all
lodged in our cells of disbelief, locked away in miserable high-rise
towers where we waited for the sands in the hourglass to finally
run out.

I opened the book again, and picked up where I had left
off...

Now, you must find the will.

When you return to the looking glass, see your-self, return to yourself, trust that you will know what to do. But you must also know that it will cost you everything. The life you've lived, the love you've known, the world you inhabit... all these will be the cost of helping the young woman in your mirror. That is because all you have done and known and created has, ultimately, come at the cost of her future; the future she might have had, the future she should have had, the future she must have, if your world is to be saved.

Beneath this text was an illustration. I recognized it as an ouroboros, a snake devouring its own tail. But this one was drawn as a sort of many-stranded Möbius strip, and like Escher's depictions of multidimensional stairways and columns, it made my head hurt to try to sort out what I was seeing. Beneath the illustration was the caption:

"It matters not how straight the gate,
how charged with punishments the scroll.
I am the master of my fate,
I am the captain of my soul."

Of course I knew the verse – the final lines of *Invictus*, by William Ernest Henley. I knew it because I had memorized it as a little girl. I would recite it to myself in bed at night, the closest thing I knew to a prayer, growing up in an atheist household.

I stopped again, my chest tight, breath short. This... damned... book! It knew about this poem, my prayer. It knew that to me, the poem represented everything that I was desperately try-ing to deny with each page I turned: that only I had control over the outcome of my life. That I owned it. No matter what I faced, no matter how well or poorly I acquitted myself, for good or for bad, I owned it. And yet. There was the girl in the mirror, lost and alone on the other side of the yawning gulf that was my life, the life I made, the one I claimed. My life without her, without her unborn child.

I knew then that I would do anything to change that. I didn't know how, but I was pretty sure the book held the answer, if there was one. It must. Otherwise, why would Alan give it to me? Even though his story was different, surely there was something in it that gave him hope that he could change things in his past. I needed to talk to him, needed him to tell me I was right, that there was a way back.

Looking up, I saw that it was time for our lunch break, so I stepped into my bathroom and quickly splashed cold water on my face to erase the evidence that the stupid book had once again brought me to tears. Wouldn't be good to appear in front of Big Nurse looking weepy. That would be a good way to earn a quick trip to the infirmary for yet another variety of happy zombie pills.

I stepped into the hall, expecting to see Alan emerging from his room, but he wasn't there yet. I glanced around quickly, to see several other inmates shuffling out of their doors and along the hall toward the elevator, but no sign of Alan. Also, no sign yet of hall monitors, so I stepped up to #332 and knocked quickly on the door. No response, no sounds from the other side. I knocked again, a little louder.

"What are you doing, Ms. Winters?" A Matron had snuck up behind me and was looming over my shoulder. Still no answer from Alan.

I turned to face the hall monitor and tried not to sound like a naughty child. "I was checking on my neighbor." It wouldn't do to admit we had anything like a friendship, which was actively discouraged.

"Your neighbor? In 332?" she replied like a mindless mynah bird. I nodded. She cocked her head. Not a mynah, I decided. A mean old crow, beady eyes and all.

"There is no one in this room, Ms. Winters. Hasn't been anyone in this room since before you came to live here."

I stared at her as if she were speaking a foreign language. "No one here?" My voice quavered in spite of me. "But what about Alan? I just saw him this morning." The head cocked in the other direction. "I mean, I saw him at breakfast," I added quickly.

Matron smiled then, a horrific baring of teeth punctuated by prominent canines. She clapped a large hand on my shoulder, holding it in a vice grip that made me wince.

"Of course you did, Ms. Winters," she fairly cooed. "Come with me, and you can tell Dr. Kallus all about it."

"No!" I twisted out of her grip and turned back to pound on the door.

"Stop that!" Matron commanded, glancing around to see that the inmates shuffling along the hall to lunch had stopped and were watching us. "Here, Winters," she dropped any hint of respect with the honorific. "See for yourself."

She placed her palm on the lock-pad next to Alan's door, and it clicked open. She swung the door inward to reveal Alan's room. Well, what had been Alan's room when I was there an hour before. Now, it was empty. Not empty like Alan had already headed down to the lunchroom. Empty like Alan had never been there. Empty like no one had been there, maybe ever. The bed was stripped, bare closets stood open, and there was a musty, unused smell to the place.

"Satisfied?" the old crow hissed.

I thought fast. Whatever was going on, I could not let her take me to the infirmary. They would dope me up and I wouldn't be able to remember anything. I knew it was absolutely critical that I remember everything – especially Alan, especially the book.

The things that were real. The things they would take from me, if I let them.

"Oh, my!" I stammered. "Of course. I'm such a silly old woman. I've mixed it up with the room across the hall!"

The room across the hall from Alan was occupied by a much older fellow named Carl, known to step outside the lines whenever he could. Actually, Alan and I liked him. He made us laugh, when little in this place could do that. Now I spotted him just down the hall, where our commotion had caused him to stop and watch with interest.

"It was that fellow!" I said loudly, pointing. "He promised me his pudding!"

Matron quickly closed the door to 332, and glanced around furtively, as if hoping no other staff were lurking nearby. I was counting on the fact that she would rather *not* have to report that anything was remotely amiss on her watch. That, and the hope that Carl would play along.

"Why, that I did," Carl said in a loud southern drawl. "Cain't abide the stuff!" He put his arm out and I hurried along to take it, as both of us headed for the elevator.

"None of that!" Matron squawked. "Keep your hands to yourselves! And no food sharing. You eat what you get, you hear?" she called from behind us.

Carl gave my hand on his arm a little squeeze before dropping it, turning back to give a brisk salute to Matron as we re-treated. "Yes, ma'am." He turned and wagged a finger in my face, and said loudly, "No pudding for you!"

I was shaking as we rode the elevator down. Carl leaned in and asked quietly, "What was that all about? How come you got that ol' biddy to open up that empty room next to you? You fixin' to move?"

I looked up at his kind face. I felt light-headed. "Empty room?"

"Yeah, that one across from me."

"Do you know... I mean, was there anyone there before? In that room?" I asked.

"Mighta been at some time. I never saw no one in that one though. Anyway, I don't know why you'd wanna go to all the trouble of switching. They're each one just as dismal as the other."

I gave him a faint smile. "Yes, they are that. I just... I thought that one might be different."

There was no point in trying to explain. My heart ached and I felt sick. My thoughts whirled like a trapped animal. *No escape, no escape. Yesterday upon the stair, I saw a man who wasn't there. He wasn't there again today... How in God's name did he get away?*

Maybe I did need the doc to up my meds.

* * *

I managed to choke down some lunch, all the while scanning the dining tables for some glimpse of Alan, hoping against hope. He clearly was not here, and as far as I could tell without raising too much curiosity, no one had any memory of him being here. So where was he, and why did I remember him if no one else did?

I stayed at the table as long as I could so as not to raise suspicion by an extra-early departure, then slipped away, handing my pudding to Carl as I left. He held the pudding up, looking at me with a raised eyebrow. I laughed. "Never could stand the stuff," I said. "Thanks for your help, anyway."

Back on the third floor, I hurried to my room, trying not to look at the door of the empty room next door. I could still smell the musty, unused smell, hear a distorted echo of Matron's ugly squawk, "There's no one in this room, Ms. Winters. Never has been. Never here. Nevermore!"

I quickly ducked into my room, terrified for a moment that I would find it, too, empty and unlived-in. But it was unchanged, the same sad cell, occupied by the same inmate. I leaned my back against the door as if I could keep out the knowledge that had already come in with me. The hard door against my shoulder blades was somehow reassuring. It was real. It was there. I was real. My ugly little room was real, with its red Formica dinette table and two matching vinyl chairs. And the cookie was real. The Petit Beurre cookie that Alan gave me. I had brought it with me from Alan's room and set it on the table to enjoy later. It was still there, and it was real! Which meant it was *all* real, and I wasn't crazy.

The book! The book was real, too. I looked around for it – not on the table, not on the nightstand, not on the bed. Under the pillow? Under the faded coverlet? On the floor. I began to panic. If I couldn't find the book...

And then I looked in the bathroom, on top of the toilet, and there it was. Right where I set it when I came in to wash my face before lunch. I had never been so happy to see anything in my life. Its dark red leather cover with its provocative title called to me anew: *What If?*

What if this were all part of the book's "pliable possibility of the past"? Why should this weird turn be any less believable than all the other Möbius twists the book had so far presented? I grabbed it and hugged it to my chest, and as I did, I had a clear image of the road in the wood, forking in different directions. Which road had Alan taken?

I carried the book over to the little table and placed it next to the cookie. Now there were two things, two solid things that confirmed Alan had been here. All I had to do was figure out which bend he had disappeared around, and I could find him. I hoped.

With a sigh, I picked up the book, and nearly dropped it again when something fell out from between its pages. It was several sheets of paper, folded in half, covered with writing on both sides. I opened it and read:

Dear Sylvia,

If you are reading this without me, you will know that it works. I followed my story from the book, and you must do the same. I didn't get to tell you about my friend, the one I told you I had denied, the story that is in the book for me. It isn't an easy story for me to tell, but it is important for you to know.

Wait... nothing about where he went or why? Or *how?* I smacked the speckled red Formica with my palm, barely missing the cookie. No, nothing that immediately useful. Instead, I was to read about the story of his childhood friend, Craig.

Craig Candler was my best friend. We had been together at a private all-boys boarding school from the time we were in third grade, back when private schooling hadn't yet been abolished by the State. We were both from well-positioned families that could afford to – and still get away with – sending their kids to elite private schools. Both of us felt alienated from our families – which tends to happen when they send you away to live at a school not fifty miles from the family manse.

When we were twelve, we both got very inter-ested in science, and our favorite teacher, Mr. January, was happy to provide us with special projects after class. We thought it was because we were both good students and he wanted to encourage us. Unfortunately, it was rather the oldest and saddest story ever told, as it turned out Mr. J was a child predator who set his sights on Craig and started inviting him for "special tutoring" sessions.

I knew something was wrong with Craig when it started. He stopped laughing, his grades went to hell, he was angry and withdrawn, even with me. I asked him what was going on, but he wouldn't talk, told me to shut up. So one evening, I decided to go to see Mr. J about it, to see if he knew what was up. Yes, I really was that naive. Remember, I was twelve at the time. Anyway, I went to the first-floor teachers' wing, and I could see the light was on in Mr. J's office, so I walked up to the door, gave a knock, and opened it. I don't want to, and don't think I need to, describe the scene I walked in on. Craig was crying, Mr. J was holding him, yelling. We all froze for a second when I opened the door, then Mr. J let go of Craig and yelled, "Get out!" And then he said if either of us said anything, they'd never believe us, and he'd make sure our families would never want anything to do with us again.

I want to say, "I was just twelve, he was an adult and a teacher, and I was scared, and I didn't know for sure what was going on." I did say that, all of it, over and over to myself. But even I never believed it was the whole truth.

Craig tried to talk to me about it, but I told him I didn't ever want to talk about it, ever. Somehow, I made it his fault that it had happened, that I had walked in on it. I knew neither of those things were true, but I clung to my lies. Even when Craig went to the dean and told him what had happened, and the dean called me in to find out if it was true. Even when my parents were contacted, and they asked me if it was true. Even at the closed-door meeting with the dean, and my parents, and Craig's parents, and Mr. January, and they heard Craig's story, and asked me if it was true. I denied it, I denied my friend. I wanted nothing more than to put the whole thing in my past and forget it had ever happened.

Ultimately, Craig was given a disciplinary warning for filing false accusations, and his family was threatened with legal action if anything was ever made public. Meanwhile, the school quietly transferred Mr. J to another of their institutions, and it was not spoken of again. Until the night, a few months later, when I returned to the room I still shared with Craig to find he had died of a drug overdose. Craig didn't do drugs, but he had told me his family medicine cabinet was full of them. The police found empty bottles that had held prescriptions for his mother, older sister, and an aunt who lived with them. They said the combination would have been lethal and fast. They also found the note he left. With no public record of events, the cops didn't know what it meant. But I did, and I knew it was for me. It said, "You knew."

I let the letter drop to land on the open, red-bound book. Unshed tears created glittering reflections around the aluminum sides of the table. I blinked, and the tears fell onto my open hands, palms-up in my lap. I began, at last, to understand that each of us, Alan and I, had lived false lives, each of us with an un-spoken, unrepented death on our hands. This must be why we had been connected by the book. But there must be more to the story. There was more to the letter, so I picked it up and read on.

> *Now you know, too, my friend. Not the sorry de-tails of my sad story, but the need you and I share for redemption, the thing that brought us to-gether, and our shared contribution to this world. But what you don't know is, our redemption, our contributions, are inextricably linked. And where they intersect, the place where each of us di-verged from our true path, and the place where we and our world can be knit together, is a great point of power. Read on, Sylvia. Read, and be-lieve, and persevere.*

> *By the way, here is my stanza of the poem:*

> *Beyond this place of wrath and tears*
> *Looms but the Horror of the shade,*
> *And yet the menace of the years*
> *Finds and shall find me unafraid.*

> *We can do this!*

> *Much love,*
> *"Deucey"*

I wiped the tears off my face, then wiped my wet palms on my sweatpants. Alan was real, and I was real, no matter how much the world we had created with our wrong turns continued to try to erase us. I determined that as long as I remembered him, Alan could not be erased. And I prayed that as long as he remembered me, wherever he was, I would continue to exist and matter, too; and our *choices* would matter.

If the book was to be believed, and Alan clearly believed it, not even the obstinate river of Time could take away our ability to choose. It might carry us far from the banks of earlier days where we left the footprints of our presence. But if we could somehow navigate its contrarian waters back to the estuary, and arrive anew at our point of embarkation, we might find the erosions carved by earlier decisions washed away. What if we *could* make a new path across that clean bank? I had to try, for Alan's sake, and mine, and the sake of pudding-loving Carl across the hall, and even — God willing — for the sake of Big Nurse and all her Matron cronies.

I pulled the book over, still open to the page with the ouroboros illustration, the same place where Alan's letter had been, and reread the instructions in the last paragraph:

> *...return to the looking glass, see yourself, return*
> *to yourself, trust that you will know what to do.*

I tucked Alan's letter into the pocket of my sweatpants, and carried the book into the bathroom, laying it open on the edge of the sink. I read again the final words from *Invictus*... "I am the master of my fate, I am the captain of my soul." I looked into the mirror and saw my reflection. Master? Captain? No; I saw a grey-haired, careworn septuagenarian, with saggy jowls and heavy eyelids. Same old woman who always stared back at me from this dimly silvered glass. But was she? I looked more deeply, and recognized in that face the ravages of hopelessness, like an increased gravity dragging her down as if she struggled to stand on an alien world. This weight, this weakness, was an acquired thing, not a part of the woman I was, the woman I am.

I looked more deeply into the mirror, looked for the woman I must believe could save herself, and her world, from the fate of this room; a fate of isolation, despair, and disempowerment. I squared my shoulders, straightened my spine - noting with satisfaction that I still could stand straight - and met my false image of frailty with compassion and strength. I saw the fear in her eyes. I understood it, but I no longer felt it, was no longer controlled by it. Alan's quoted verse *...the menace of the years finds, and shall find me, unafraid...* shimmered before me. I knew myself as this woman, the one who faced me now, and I knew what I needed to do. I needed to give this strength, this compassion to the young girl I had been, alone and frightened on the other side of the looking glass.

I looked for her now, beyond and within my elder reflection, and her soft round features and searching eyes appeared once more before me. I felt myself drawn to her. I moved toward her, moved through her somehow, and found myself suddenly on the other side, a kindly old woman standing behind her, looking over her shoulder at their dual reflection in the mirror.

* * *

Suddenly, I caught the reflection of an old lady standing behind me, looking over my shoulder. I gasped and spun around, knocking the pregnancy test stick off the sink, where it landed with a clatter on the pink and black floor tiles. I clapped my hand over my mouth to stifle the scream I could feel rising in my throat. The last thing in the world I wanted was for my mom to come running into the bathroom to see what was wrong with me. That thought scared me more than a stranger suddenly appearing behind me.

189

She raised her hands and made gentle shushing sounds. She spoke quietly, thank goodness. "It's okay. You're alright. I'm here to help you, Sylvia, not hurt you." Her voice sounded somehow familiar – like my mom, or one of my aunts?

"Who are you? How did you get in here?" I hissed.

"You can call me Trip. I can't really explain how I got here, but I can tell you why I'm here."

There was something about her, something that made me trust her... or at least want to. "Okay. Spill."

A little smile played at the corner of her mouth. "I'm here because of this," she said, leaning over to pick up the pregnancy test and holding it out to me. I would just as soon have grabbed a live viper from her hand, but I took it and stuck it into the pocket of my jeans.

She continued, "I know what you're going through, and I know no one else knows. And I know what you're thinking about doing. I also know that you don't really want to do it."

I clamped my jaws shut to keep from crying. Didn't do any good, tears just ran down my cheeks anyway. "How do you know anything about it?" I grumbled through gritted teeth.

"I know because I've been where you are. Exactly where you are. And I know how you feel. More importantly, I know two things that I wish I had known when I was your age: One, you are strong enough to do this, to have your baby."

I felt myself wince when she said it that way. My... baby. It was the first time I'd heard it out loud, or even thought about it that way. But of course, it was... my baby.

"Two things," I said, trying to regain control. "You said you know two things. What else?"

The old lady stepped forward, holding out her hands. For some reason – maybe because I was feeling so alone or scared, I don't know – I took her hands. I needed to.

"The other thing I know is that if you do not have your

baby, you will never forgive yourself. And living with that will be a weight of guilt and shame that will far outlive the temporary shame you'll face in admitting you're pregnant."

I looked deeply into her eyes, and unlike when I looked in the mirror, I couldn't see any blame there. I couldn't see any fear. Only strength and certainty. And love.

Oh, my God - I actually have a Fairy Godmother. No wings, no wand, no gossamer gown - just an old lady in baggy sweats and sneakers. Just my luck.

She squeezed my hands gently, and said, "I know. It feels impossible, but I am here to help you. And I know you can do it. Do you trust me?"

I don't know why - my rational brain was obviously taking a nap somewhere in a back room - but I did. I trusted her more than I had ever trusted anyone - even myself.

"Alright," I said. "I'll do it." I dropped her hands and turned back to the mirror. "I'm going to be a mom," I whispered, and the old lady in the mirror behind me smiled a very familiar smile.

* * *

She had been right about everything, and whenever I became frightened and overwhelmed and wanted to give up, I had only to look for her reflection behind me in my mirror, looking over my shoulder, encouraging and supporting me with a look full of all the certainty I lacked. *I can do this.*

The last time I saw Trip - if I ever truly saw her - was in the little mirror above the sink in my hospital room, as I held my newborn infant daughter, whose perfect little face was framed by a crown of curls so thick and dark that she might have been wearing a wig. To think that I might have lost this precious child, might have given in to fear and shame... I remembered Trip's words, then: "If you do not have your baby, you will never forgive yourself," and I knew she had been right.

191

In the looking glass world behind me, my Fairy God-mother smiled. "What will you name her?" she asked.

Her image in the mirror shimmered as my eyes filled with grateful tears. "I'm going to name her after you," I said.

She laughed, a so-familiar laugh. "You're going to name her Trip?"

"No, I'm going to call her Angel. Because you have been a guardian angel to me, and without you, she wouldn't be here."

Over my shoulder, I saw her smile transform her face, as if she had taken a youth elixir. She still reminded me so much of someone, but I never could place just who. I looked down at my round-cheeked baby with pride and gratitude, and when I looked up again, Trip was gone.

* * *

On screen, an elaborately coiffed interviewer, impeccably dressed in a peach-colored dress that perfectly complemented her cocoa-colored complexion, looked into the camera and announced, "Good evening, friends. I'm Kaitlin Thompson, and this is America Based." On the screen, as the show's theme music swelled, the America Based intro animation played, then faded to be replaced by a wider shot of the show's host that included her guest – me, a two-term President of the United States, now reduced to a bundle of nerves as I faced America's favorite on-screen personality to tell my story. Seeing myself framed in the monitor next to my elegant interviewer, all I could think was that I hoped my dark blue suit and white blouse wouldn't look dowdy next to her lush peach ensemble. Funny how things like that start to bother you when you reach a certain age.

Kaitlin continued, "Tonight, seven years after surviving an assassination attempt and being sworn in for her second term, President Angel Coleman joins us to talk about her life and time in office, and her newly released memoir. Welcome, President Coleman."

"Thank you, Kaitlin," I replied. "I'm delighted to be able to share my story with your audience, and with the world."

"You are very forthcoming in your book, President Coleman, giving us real insight into your life, who you are. To start with, you were born to a single teenage mother, being adopted by her new husband when you were five years old."

"Yes, that is something I have always shared in my public life, with my parents' blessing." I looked offstage to where Mom and Dad were sitting side by side, most likely holding hands. Although I couldn't really see them for the glare of the studio lights, I could feel their love and pride surrounding me.

I continued, "Their strength and commitment in making hard choices and standing up for what's right, for those without a voice, gave me the courage to believe that I could do the same. That's what led me into public life."

Kaitlin smiled warmly. "That was certainly not the easy path, Madam President, but having made that choice, you have uniquely stayed true to your convictions throughout your years of service. And you never allowed the 'bludgeonings of chance,' as the poem says, to deter you."

She glanced down at the notecards she held in her hands, as if she needed a reminder before resuming. I suspected she only had them for effect, as she looked back up at me with her famous sea-green eyes, and continued, "You tackled some of the toughest problems we have faced as a nation – plummeting birthrates, dissolution of families, precipitous crime rates, erosion of personal liberties, just to name a few. What drove you to attempt what many before you had, frankly, run away from?"

I met her piercing look with my own unwavering regard. "I wouldn't have deserved the trust of the American people if I had the opportunity and the position to do something about those things, and didn't do my best. If they wanted someone to take the easy path, they would have voted in any of my opponents. But they didn't, they trusted me to take the high road – the road less traveled, if we're quoting poetry. My parents and my upbringing gave me the strength to do that." I laughed, and added honestly, "And I couldn't have faced my parents if I had done less."

Kaitlin smiled wryly and nodded. "We all need people who hold us accountable, and voters don't always do that."

"Sadly true," I agreed.

"These were tough issues, certainly, but in your book you talk about the hardest problem you tackled was widespread child trafficking. Can you tell us more about that?"

I shifted in my chair and sat up as straight as possible, trying not to squint against the glaring studio lights. I wanted to hit this one head-on, no fear, no hesitation. "Yes, Kaitlin. That battle required all the strength I could muster, and all the support I could gather. First, I had to pray for the stamina to face it. I had to stare in the Gorgon's face, and not be immobilized by the horror of it. And I had to get others to do the same. Until we all saw it for what it was, we couldn't fight it. Then, we had to fight the traffickers, and the power behind them – including very highly placed politicians, business moguls, celebrities. And making people look *that* horror in the face was even harder."

"In your book you talk about having a close advisor you depended on through this process," Kaitlin prompted.

"Yes, one of my closest, most trusted advisors, Craig Candler," I replied. "Also a lifelong friend of my family. He and my father were at school together when they were boys."

Though I couldn't see Dad past the lights, I could feel his encouragement, and his lifelong advice echoed with me, steadying me. *"Don't ever be embarrassed or afraid when it comes to telling the truth, Angel-baby. Even an ugly truth gives its teller all the strength needed to carry it into the light. Tell the truth, never deny it, then let it travel its own path."*

I continued, "While they were at school together, Craig

was sexually molested by one of their teachers. My father was a witness. The school and the teacher attempted to deny it, said the boys were making it up. But they stood up to the school, and with both of them testifying against him, the predator was fired and prosecuted for his crimes. And I say crimes, because when the truth came out, it gave other boys the courage to tell their stories, as well. Turned out the teacher in question had done this before, to other boys."

"It must have taken a lot of courage, for those boys to stand up like that," Kaitlin commented. I thought she might be in the running for Master of Understatement, but I guess smoothing out the rough edges was part of her job description.

She continued, prompting, "So the boys remained friends all their lives. Your dad even named him as your Godfather, and ultimately, as you say, he became one of your advisors when you became President."

"That's right, Kaitlin. His experience at school had motivated him to pursue a career in fighting child sexual abuse and human trafficking. That, and my personal trust and regard for him, made him the perfect advisor to help me fight those things during my Presidency."

Kaitlin leaned in a little with her next question, "And this is also the man who saved your life from a would-be assassin?"

I nodded, while I swallowed the lump rising in my throat. "Yes. Craig was next to me on the dais as I was being sworn in for my second term. Suddenly, we heard someone shout, 'He's got a gun!' I saw the Secret Service agents lunge toward the crowd, heard a shot. I thought they had managed to get the gunman, until Craig slumped against me. He had stepped in front of me just as the gunman fired. He gave his life to save mine."

"You give him credit for saving a lot of lives, in your book," Kaitlin commented.

"Yes, I do, because without his guidance and strength,

which I carried with me to complete our work in my second term, thousands of children would still be locked in underground tunnels, traded between the mansions of truly evil people, kidnapped, tortured, sold, and killed. By the thousands, Kaitlin. Those are the lives that Craig saved, along with mine."

"I think you do a great job of telling their stories, and Craig's, and yours, in your book. I highly recommend it to my viewers. It is real and unflinching and brave, and leaves your readers with a lot to think about," Kaitlin said. "A lot of public figures write their memoirs – some in recent history seemed to feel their autobiographies were interesting enough to warrant four or five volumes!"

I smiled. "Hopefully, in my case one will be sufficient."

"Yours is definitely different," Kaitlin replied. "It manages to avoid justification, gilding, and preening. You just tell your story, good choices, bad choices, warts and all, and along the way, you get us to look at our own lives in the same way, as painful as that can be. Can you tell us about how you came to write it, this memoir?"

"Thank you, Kaitlin, that's high praise. I hope readers will share your enthusiasm. But really, I felt compelled to tell the story, to tie all my choices – the crossroads and intersections of my life – to their results and resolves. It's not meant to be a cautionary tale, just an accounting, you might say, of will and consequences. I wrote it to answer the question that always arises for me in watershed moments of my life, the question we must be open to, if we are going to make the world better with our choices."

"This question?" The interviewer flashed her flawless smile as she held up a copy of my newly published book, with its dark red leather-like binding, its title shining in gold script embossed across the cover:

"What If?"